Had her identity be

Everyone believed she was dead. If someone knew she was really Melody Garner, what did they have to lose by killing her for real?

"You all right?"

She looked at Luke and found concerned eyes staring back.

He directed his gaze back to the road, a frown firmly in place. "I shouldn't have hired you as a nanny. Or anyone to watch the kids. This is my fault. I should've known I could put you in danger."

"What? No." She wanted to tell Luke the truth. Tell him everything. Not having anyone—no family, coworkers, a significant other or anyone—was excruciating. "We don't even know who's targeting us. Or if someone is after the kids or just me."

"I appreciate you saying so, but I doubt anyone would be after you unless it has to do with you working for me. Why would anyone want to hurt you?"

How could she answer? If she told him the truth, would he tell the rest of the Rangers? How long until everyone knew she was alive? Was she ready to take the chance?

Until recently, **Connie Queen** has spent all of her life in Texas, where she met and married her high school sweetheart. Together they've raised eight children and are enjoying their grandchildren. Today she resides with her husband and Nash, her Great Dane, in Nebraska, where she's working on her next heart-throbbing suspense.

Book by Connie Queen

Love Inspired Suspense

Justice Undercover

JUSTICE UNDERCOVER

CONNIE QUEEN

LOVE INSPIRED SUSPENSE
INSPIRATIONAL ROMANCE

LOVE INSPIRED®SUSPENSE
INSPIRATIONAL ROMANCE

Recycling programs
for this product may
not exist in your area.

ISBN-13: 978-1-335-40289-9

Justice Undercover

Copyright © 2020 by Connie Queen

This edition published by arrangement with Harlequin Books S.A.

For questions and comments about the quality of this book, please contact us at CustomerService@Harlequin.com.

Love Inspired
22 Adelaide St. West, 40th Floor
Toronto, Ontario M5H 4E3, Canada
www.Harlequin.com

Printed in U.S.A.

Mercy and truth are met together; righteousness
and peace have kissed each other.
–Psalms 85:10

For Bruce...my husband, real-life hero and biggest fan.
My kids...Jeb, Andi, Connor, Cooper, Jessi, JP, Savannah
and Hayden, every one of you is special.
A lady couldn't ask for a better family and cheer team.

To Tina James, my editor—
thanks for believing in my work. I'm so thrilled
you welcomed me into the Love Inspired family.

To my mentor, Tina Radcliffe, for making me
use my emotions even when I didn't want to.

To all my unbelievably supportive critique partners,
past and present, who have trudged through horrible
first drafts, endless typos and rejections. Lana, Angie,
Rhona, Sharee, Sherrinda and Jackie.

Thank you to my writing sisters
for your continual encouragement.

God bless you all.

ONE

Kylie Stone glanced over her shoulder, unable to shake the feeling she was being watched. No one was there except an elderly couple feeding the flamingos. No suspicious person lurking nearby.

Would the day ever come when she could truly relax? Or a day when she wouldn't think about the sweet mother and two precious children that had perished under her care in the Witness Protection Program?

It'd been three long years since she had disappeared, abandoning her job at the United States Marshals Service, and had become Kylie Stone.

The huge Texas flag waved lazily in the warm afternoon breeze, and a red bird hopped from limb to limb in the pecan tree above. By all appearances, everything was peaceful at Rocky Creek Zoo.

The uneasiness still lingered. Her instincts were normally spot-on. Maybe they should've stayed home today. She held out her hands. "Time to go."

"No," two-year-old fraternal twins, Braden and Zoe, cried in unison.

"Now, come on. I told you we were leaving after we saw George." The gorilla knuckle-walked across his spacious enclosure and climbed up a large leaning tree. He wasn't nearly as interested in the children as they were in him.

Kylie dropped down to one knee between the blond-haired, blue-eyed sweethearts. "Tell him 'bye."

"Unca Luke is coming."

Zoe's hopeful expression twisted Kylie's gut. A glance at her smart watch told her their uncle, Texas Ranger Luke Dryden, was almost ninety minutes late. She couldn't wait any longer for him to join them. "It's time to go." She gave them both a quick peck on the head. "Don't forget we have cookies waiting for us."

The twins reluctantly waved to the five-hundred-pound gorilla. "Bye-bye."

Kylie fastened the toddlers into the stroller and surveyed her surroundings once more. Then, when she was satisfied no one was there, they headed toward the exit.

Braden glanced up, his expression hopeful. "Too-kie."

"When we get home," Kylie told him and continued moving quickly.

"Two too-kies." Braden kicked his cowboy boots against the footrest. "One for Unca Luke."

Kylie smiled, not wanting to discourage the toddlers, but their uncle had worked late almost every night since Kylie had been babysitting for him. Being in law enforcement, she knew, made it difficult to be a single parent with his niece and nephew, but he needed to find more time.

Zoe stared silently into her lap. Kylie wished she'd show half the enthusiasm as her brother. She didn't know whether the girl had always been shy, or the quietness was brought on by the loss of her mother.

The Ranger had agreed to take off early today to meet them at the small city zoo for the afternoon. He'd texted a couple of hours ago that he'd be late. Since then, they had already seen all the exhibits once, some twice, and now the twins were missing their naps.

If she was a real nanny, she would've set their uncle straight from the beginning and let him know she wouldn't stay late. But she had sought this job in hopes of getting closer to Luke, so she could learn if there was a connection between the death of the Texas Ranger's sister and Hal Alcott, the man who'd killed Kylie's witness and made it clear on that fateful day three years ago that he intended to kill her, as well.

So far, she hadn't found a link.

The nanny service had warned her that Luke had gone through two previous sitters the month before she took the job, and he had been fined multiple times for being late.

She returned the rented double stroller to the self-serve island and grabbed her backpack. Holding the twins' hands, they exited between two giant giraffe statues on the way to the almost empty parking lot.

Kylie assessed the perimeter before they stepped onto the sidewalk.

Her gaze narrowed on the rusty minivan parked next to her blue Jeep Cherokee in the second row. Her breath hitched as she studied the vehicle. A woman sat behind the wheel. The van backed out and left, little heads bobbing in the back seat. Just a mom and kids. A smile spread across her lips. She was extra jumpy today.

"Carry me." Zoe wiggled out of her grasp and thrust her tiny hands in the air.

She gathered the little girl into her arms and gave

her a slight squeeze, savoring the closeness. She missed protecting families. Missed her job.

The protective instincts were difficult to hide after years of service. No one knew her identity, and evidently, no one was after these kids. To everyone around her, Kylie was simply the nanny.

She took Braden's hand once more. "Come on, let's go."

The boy took leaping steps, never seeming to tire.

Luke Dryden's white pickup pulled in at the far end of the premises and stopped at the parking attendant's booth. Finally. At least he would be able to share cookies and spend a little time with the children today.

Relieved at seeing his truck, she almost didn't notice the silver SUV barreling down the lane toward them. Warning bells went off in her brain as fear crawled up her spine. This wasn't just a guy ignoring the fifteen-mile-per-hour speed zone. She picked up Braden, and with a child in each arm, ran for her vehicle as fast as she could manage.

The SUV came to a screeching halt as she reached the Jeep. Time slowed as her heart raced—she needed a weapon.

Kylie set down the kids next to her vehicle and pulled a hairbrush from the backpack. "Stay here."

A hefty man jumped out of the SUV and rushed toward her. Curly brown hair protruded from under a red baseball cap. Though he didn't have a visible weapon, her heart seized. On impulse, Kylie dropped the backpack and put her hand on top of Braden's head to make sure he stayed behind her.

"Ky-ee," Braden yelled.

Please, God, help me protect these kids.

The attacker's gray eyes connected with hers and there was triumph in his gaze, before he swung a fist.

She slapped down his punch while simultaneously stepping forward to generate more power as she struck him in the jaw with the blunt end of the hairbrush. His head snapped back, a curse blasting from his lips, but he didn't go down.

He was large and slow. Before he could recover, she advanced and executed a sharp jab to his ribs.

"Ugh." He bent over, wrapping his arms around his middle.

The kids cried and clung to the back of her capris.

She regripped the brush and eyed him, noting the disbelief in his expression. Gently shoving the twins behind her once more, Kylie stepped forward with her left foot and put her arms in an on-guard position, ready to strike again.

"You think you're pretty tough," he shouted. "Well, stop this." He whipped a KA-BAR knife from his waistband.

Tires squealed. A blur of white flashed to her right, but she kept her eyes trained on the man in the red hat, prepared in case he decided to throw the knife. He turned, scrambled into his SUV and peeled out of the lot.

"Are you okay?" Luke Dryden's baritone voice boomed through his open door.

"Yes." But, of course, she wasn't. Her voice was shaky, and her chest heaved with each runaway breath. She willed her body to stop trembling. The kids were crying, but safe.

Luke grabbed his cell phone. "I need backup. Possible attempted child abduction…" The words drifted away as he slammed the door and took off in pursuit of the SUV.

Kylie picked up the kids. "It's okay. Don't cry."

"Unca Luke…" Braden's lip puckered, and he held out his hands toward the disappearing truck.

"He'll be back, honey." She clung to the little fellow. She had saved them. This time. What if she couldn't the next time? What if, just like the Coffey family, she failed to protect them? Another family would be devastated.

"Scary bad man." Braden's face scrunched. "Me don't like him."

Still trembling from the close call, Kylie pulled the twins closer. "Me, neither. Everything's going to be all right."

Minutes later, Luke pulled back into the parking lot and stopped beside her Jeep. Decked out in his Texas Ranger attire of jeans, white shirt and red tie, he took the frightened kids from her and pulled them into his arms.

Kylie's own arms dropped to her side, and she relaxed her stance. After all, she was just the nanny.

"He got away." Luke Dryden had wanted to continue pursuit of the Tahoe, but fear for the twins' safety won out. Anger pulsed through his veins, but he reined in his emotions for the kids' sakes. They were upset enough. Megan's kids. His sister hadn't been gone three months and already he was failing as a guardian. Every muscle in his body tensed as he thought of how easily he could've lost them.

"Are you two okay?" he asked. Tears lined Braden's blue eyes, but at least he'd stopped crying. Zoe continued to sob even as Luke held her close. "It's okay, Zoe girl. Uncle Luke's got you."

Had the man been after the twins or Kylie?

His gaze landed on his nanny—she had a hairbrush clutched in her hand and her face was red. Sweat beaded above her lip. Her breathing was still not quite back to normal. "Did you know that guy?"

Kylie licked her lips as though she was considering the matter. "No, I didn't recognize him. I saw you pull into the lot, but then this SUV came speeding toward us. I didn't know what else to do except try to get the kids in the vehicle. But I didn't have time."

"Did you hit him with that?"

She fidgeted with the brush. "Uh, yeah."

"I'm glad the man didn't have a weapon." He stared at her as the kids settled their heads on his shoulders.

"He pulled a knife, but thankfully you drove up and scared him off before he could use it."

"I didn't need to hear that." Luke shook his head.

At barely five feet, she wasn't as big as a mite. She had big eyes and a high-pitched voice. She looked scared, but something in her expression caused him to doubt his initial analysis. Dressed in a pink T-shirt and denim capris, she appeared sweet, and non-threatening. His dad would've called her cute as a button. His gaze went back to the brush. She hadn't screamed. That's what was bothering him. Her cool confidence. When she'd swung at the guy, he thought *she* was the one with a knife. "A brush? Really?"

The corners of her mouth lifted slightly, and a dimple formed. "I didn't have anything else. I thank God I even thought of it." Grabbing the backpack from the pavement, she quickly stuffed the brush inside.

"Nice job" was all Luke could say. He didn't reply to the God comment. It wasn't that he didn't believe in God, or was even mad at Him for not saving his sister. His faith, though, wavered. Guilt tugged at him, but no matter how much he prayed, his faith seemed to be growing weaker. He simply didn't know how to get it back.

Kylie held her hands out toward the toddlers. "You want me to put them in their car seats?"

Even though Braden leaned toward Kylie, Luke pulled back, not wanting to let them go just yet. "I've got them." Zoe clung to his neck, and his chin dropped to the top of her head. He inhaled the clean scent of baby shampoo. The little girl was the image of his sister at that age. "What I need to know is…did the man attack you or was he after the kids?"

"I'm not certain. When he first jumped out of his vehicle, he eyed the twins. I felt sure his intention was to take them since he didn't go for my backpack."

Luke's chest constricted. She confirmed his speculations. The SUV had partially blocked his view and the attacker had kept his head down. Luke hadn't seen his face. "I need to call this in. Can you give me a description of this guy or what he was wearing?"

"Brown curly hair. Gray eyes. Approximately six foot and two hundred pounds. Red baseball cap. Jeans." She looked heavenward, as if trying to picture him. "Brown or beige shirt. Boots. The guy was thirtyish. The vehicle looked like a late-model silver Tahoe."

How had she recalled all those details? Most witnesses had to be coaxed into remembering. "I don't suppose you happened to notice the license-plate number, too?"

"Sorry."

He eyed her. "You sure you didn't recognize him?"

"I'm sure."

"Is there anyone who'd want to hurt you?"

She hesitated. "No."

Okay, why the uncertainty? He'd have to question her more later.

An older couple lingered on the sidewalk. Luke handed the twins to Kylie and then strode over. "Good afternoon. Did you see what happened?"

The man sporting a T-shirt that read Great Dads Get Promoted to Grandpa regarded his Ranger badge. "We walked out just as the lady hit him with the brush. I didn't get a good lo—"

"We saw her and those two adorable kids in the park several times," his silver-haired wife interrupted. "I thought that truck was going to hit them, as fast as it was traveling. What is this world coming to? Pure shame people can't enjoy an outing at the zoo without being robbed."

"Now, Earlene, you didn't see anyone get robbed."

"I didn't say they were."

Luke smiled at the couple—they reminded him of his grandparents. He took the rest of their statement and jotted down their names and phone number. There were no other people in the parking lot, so he went back to Kylie.

They buckled the kids in before he called his boss. He had only gotten the first three digits of the license plate and had called it in to Sergeant Jamison with the local police while chasing the vehicle out of the park. The sergeant put out a Be On the Lookout on the Tahoe and agreed to interview him and Kylie at home.

Using his phone, Luke snapped several pictures of the parking lot, the Jeep and the tire marks left by the Tahoe. A glance at the light poles and the corners of the building showed only one security camera at the entrance gate. He'd get the number of park security on the way out and give it to Jamison to see if the SUV was caught on tape.

He walked over to the Jeep. "I changed my mind. I want the kids in my truck. You're welcome to ride back to the house with me if you're nervous, and I can send someone to drop off your vehicle shortly."

"I'm perfectly capable of..." Kylie stopped short. "I'll take the Jeep, but I'd feel better if you'd follow me."

Kylie pulled out of the zoo with Luke Dryden following close behind. She racked her brain trying to figure out why the attacker would want the kids. Kidnapping? Even though there were reports of kidnapping rings, she'd never heard of any in this area. But why? Did today's attack tie to Megan's death?

It was Hal Alcott himself who'd killed Lori Coffey and her two children early the morning the woman was to testify. Kylie knew because she had seen Alcott as he looked over the deadly scene. It hadn't been him today, but it could've been one of his men.

Was it possible Kylie was the target? But how? No one knew she was in Rocky Creek. She hadn't told anyone. Not even her beloved boisterous family in Wichita Falls. They all believed she was dead. Killed in the line of duty. Even her sister, Tina, her best friend, didn't know she had survived.

Even though the explosion hadn't killed her, it had left her alone, with no remnants of her former life. In everything that mattered, Melody Garner had died three years ago at twenty-nine. Her Kylie-Stone self was thirty-two, with no family. Until Hal Alcott was safely behind bars, her future didn't hold much hope of changing.

Today's attacker had looked determined, so she doubted it was a case of mistaken identity. If neither she nor the children were the target, that only left Luke Dryden.

Pressing the brake, she came to a stop at a red light, a dark emotional cloud settling over her. *If* someone had learned her whereabouts, did she need to move on? Again? Four times in the last eighteen months. Would she be forced to abandon her investigation into the death of Dryden's sister?

Kylie scanned the road and nearby parking lots, but didn't see any signs of the silver SUV. Just Luke's truck behind her. She noted his intense gaze even through the tinted window. They had only had a couple of conversations that lasted more than five minutes since she'd met him. The Ranger had that professional, reserved approach that left a person wondering what was going through his mind. What would she find if she was able to peel back that stoic mask of his? Today, as he'd held Braden and Zoe after the attack, had been the first sign of affection she'd seen in the man toward the twins. But was she being fair? He had suffered with the loss of his sister, and now this. She couldn't imagine the weight he carried.

The light turned green, and she took off.

An image of Zoe and Braden helping her make chocolate-chip cookies this morning flitted through her mind. They stood on a couple of wooden chairs placed against the counter as Kylie helped them put in the ingredients. Then, like her mama used to do for Kylie and her siblings, she got three spoons and gave everyone their own sampling of dough. The twins had devoured it. A smile tugged at her mouth.

She straightened, pushing the memory away. Getting attached was not an option.

Ahead of her, traffic on the two-lane highway picked up. A school bus braked and signaled a turn. There was no turning lane, and Kylie came to a stop while the bus waited for oncoming cars to pass. When they took off once again, she glanced toward the five-and-dime store.

A silver vehicle sat in the side lot behind the trash dumpster. She couldn't tell if it was the same SUV, but since the kids were safe with the Ranger, she intended to check it out.

Using a hands-free device, she called Luke. "I'm going to stop at the store to get some milk. I'll meet you at the house. Do you need anything else while I'm there?"

As soon as he said no, she hung up and turned the Jeep around. She headed back to the store and pulled into the second drive—the one farthest away from the silver vehicle. The dumpster blocked her view, and she couldn't tell if the driver was still in the SUV or not. The license number was all she needed.

Kylie pulled around the opposite side of the building. The drive didn't circle around the store, so she eased down the lane and parked behind a bread truck. A couple of tall hedges provided a barrier between the back of the store and a row of houses. She planned to stay only long enough to get the license-plate number.

Kylie retrieved her Glock from the locked console and stepped out of her Jeep. Staying close to the brick building, she inched along the back wall until she got to the corner. She lifted her gun and peeked around the edge.

The man in the red ball cap sat inside the silver

Tahoe, staring at his phone. There were no other vehicles between her and the SUV, which meant there was no way to get close enough to read the plate without being spotted.

Panic stripped her breath away. She'd found him. Now what? Call the Ranger? He had the kids with him. Maybe she should go back to her Jeep and wait until the Tahoe went to leave, get the license-plate number and then call Luke. Where she had parked offered a great view of the exit.

Kylie started to turn away when a maroon sedan sped into the parking lot. The driver's-side window zipped down, revealing a person wearing a red ski mask. The barrel of an assault rifle stuck out the window as he took aim.

"No!" she yelled.

The man in the silver Tahoe jerked, confusion etched on his face. He looked around before he spotted the masked man. He threw the SUV into gear and peeled out in Reverse.

Pop. Pop. Pop.

Her attacker slumped forward, and his Tahoe crashed into a utility pole.

For a split second, shock held Kylie's feet in place. Her pistol was no match for the killer's powerful weapon. Through the ski mask, his eyes landed on her, their gazes locking for one fleeting moment.

Somewhere, a lady screamed.

The masked man gave her one more glance before the sedan screeched out of the parking lot.

Adrenaline surging, Kylie shoved her gun into her waistband, spun around and face-planted into a solid chest.

Luke Dryden.

TWO

"The milk is *inside* the store." Glancing around the edge of the building, he spotted the Tahoe. The man inside sagged against the steering wheel behind the shattered windshield. "What happened?"

Kylie cleared her throat. "He was shot."

Luke protectively stepped in front of his nanny, fear increasing his anger. "That's the same truck from the zoo, isn't it?"

She nodded. "The shooter sped off."

"I need you to go sit with the kids while I check this out." He didn't wait for her to answer and quickly called Sergeant Jamison. "This is Luke Dryden again. Shots fired. Shooter is gone. I need backup at the dollar store off Highway Thirteen. The victim may be fatally wounded. He's the suspect from the zoo. Checking it out now."

Luke approached the vehicle, gun ready, but the man showed no signs of life. A few people huddled on the sidewalk near the corner of the store and watched him. "Step back." He flashed his badge. "Texas Ranger."

No movement from the SUV. He glanced in the back of the vehicle to make certain no other persons were inside, then returned to the driver's side. He opened the door and felt for the man's pulse. Nothing. The man was dead.

A Rocky Creek police cruiser pulled into the parking lot, followed by an ambulance. Sergeant Jamison's black Ford Explorer trailed behind them and came to a stop. Jamison, short and muscular, put on his hat and strode toward him.

"I'm afraid it's too late for this one."

Jamison eyed Luke. "Dryden, care to tell me what's going on?"

"I'm not certain." Luke again described what occurred at the zoo, and how Kylie's attacker had now been found dead.

The sergeant looked at one of the younger officers. "White, get those plates called in ASAP and then find out if any of those people witnessed the shooting. Have Thompson tape off the crime scene until the technician gets here."

The officer nodded and went to do as he was told.

"I'll need to get a statement from your nanny," Jamison said.

"She's on the other side of the store with the twins." They went around the building and found Kylie standing outside his truck with the back door open, the kids sound asleep. She had donned a pink-and-brown Farm Girl cap, and from the corner of her eye, she glanced from him to Jamison while keeping her head downward. Luke supposed she was upset, which was understandable. He was surprised she wasn't crying, but everyone handled traumatic situations differently.

"I'd like to ask you a few questions." Jamison held a pen and pad. "Name?"

"Kylie Stone."

Luke listened as Jamison asked what happened, and she explained that she'd just walked around the side of the building and saw the man in the SUV when a car pulled into the parking lot and opened fire.

Jamison asked the question that Luke wanted the answer to. "Why were you at the back of the building, ma'am?"

She shrugged. "I saw the Tahoe and wondered if it could be the same man from the zoo."

"Don't you know better than to approach someone like that?"

"Oh, yes, sir. I understand. I had no plans to confront the man."

"Did you see the shooting?"

"I did."

A news van pulled in. Kylie turned to Luke, scratched the back of her neck and asked quietly, "May I take the kids home if you're through with me?"

"You need to finish giving Sergeant Jamison your statement."

"I ran around the back side of the building and saw the man in the Tahoe on the phone when a maroon sedan pulled into the parking lot." Kylie talked fast. "Couldn't see the license plate or the make and model, but the driver wore a red ski mask and pointed a rifle out the window and shot the guy from the zoo. Then he sped away."

A reporter headed their way with a cameraman in tow.

Her eyes met Luke's. "Sleeping in car seats just isn't the same as a bed. The kids will be cranky if they don't get a good nap. May I take them home now? I'm tired."

Was that desperation he saw? But why? Being a small department, sometimes officers were willing to give some latitude. He turned to Jamison.

"Go," the sergeant said. "We'll finish processing the scene. I can come by the house later if we have more questions."

"That'll work," Luke said.

"Thanks." Kylie hurried back into her Jeep.

As Luke followed her to his house, his stomach churned at the day's events as he was unsure of what they meant. Just like when Megan was in trouble, he'd seen danger coming but couldn't do anything to stop it. He'd tried to get Megan to open up, to tell him what was going on in her life, because he had sensed her pulling away from family and friends. No matter how hard he tried to help, he couldn't figure out what was wrong. He'd finally written off the situation as his sister simply struggling in her marriage to Tommy, and she was either too embarrassed or too absorbed with her problems to take the hand he'd offered.

Now, only three months after her death, danger was closing in again. This time, he was determined to stop it. It wasn't just that Braden and Zoe needed him to be competent, but Kylie did, too. Luke didn't know what to think about his nanny. She was like no one he'd ever met before. Cute and great with the kids. Patient. Seemed to really care about them and wanted to have fun. A natural caregiver. He shook his head. He still couldn't get the image of her fighting off the big guy with a *brush* out of his head. It wasn't uncommon for women to take self-defense classes, or maybe she had been the only girl in a houseful of brothers. He realized he didn't know much about the twins' nanny outside the background check performed by the agency, because he'd never asked.

So many lives depending on his ability to do his job. Was it coincidence on the heels of his sister's death that there was a child abduction attempt involving the twins? Megan's murder and this attack had to be connected. One thing was for certain—these people weren't kidding around. Hopefully something would come back on the license plates.

This time, he'd ask for help. He picked up his phone and called the one person he could depend on.

"O'Neill."

"I need your help."

After explaining to his coworker what had happened, O'Neill agreed to drive up and assist him in the investigation. And if there were more attacks, there was no one he would rather have by his side. Luke pulled into the long drive of his small ranch-style house feeling a tad better. Not only was Jax O'Neill one of the best Texas Rangers in the field, but he also knew the details of Megan's case.

Kylie parked under the carport while he hit the garage-door opener and waited for the door to open. He held a finger in the air to tell her he'd be right back, and then he went inside and performed a quick sweep of the house.

He came back. "Clear. Come on in."

They brought in the kids and put them in their beds. After Kylie stepped out, he stared down at the twins, their vulnerability really striking home. Zoe sucked on her thumb and snuggled her favorite pink blanket, which her grandmother had quilted. Braden sprawled out beside his Texas Ranger teddy bear. So young to have lost their mama. Their daddy, Tommy, was nowhere to be found. And now someone had tried to abduct them.

Where was Tommy? Megan had never filed a missing-person report. What kind of father left his wife and kids? Luke's dad— No, not his real dad, but even so, Sam Dryden, his stepdad, would've never abandoned his family. A lump formed in his throat, making it impossible to swallow. Maybe Luke should call his parents and let them know what was going on. Of course he should. They had the right to know.

He punched in his mom's number while still in the privacy of the bedroom.

She picked up on the first ring. "Luke. Is something wrong?"

A stab of guilt hit him in the chest. If those were the first words out of his mom's mouth, then he really should feel ashamed. "Zoe and Braden are fine, but it appears someone tried to take them from the zoo."

"Oh, no. Are they all right?"

"They're safe. I just called because I thought you deserved to know."

His dad's voice boomed in the background. "What's going on, Dottie?"

"Luke, we're coming over."

Maybe he shouldn't have called. Now his parents would worry, but there was nothing they could do. "Please don't. Kylie, my nanny, is here and the kids are safe with me."

"Are you certain? We don't mind."

Her voice tugged at his heart. He didn't like the tension that had built between them. "I've got this. I need to go."

"Please call us if we can help."

"I will." He clicked off. Megan had left Luke as the guardian of his children. He still wasn't sure why she'd chosen him. Probably because she believed she would live forever and would never need anyone to care for them.

As he walked back into the kitchen, the thought occurred to Luke that maybe Tommy hadn't left of his own free will. Or maybe, like Megan, he was dead.

Kylie shoved a plate of chocolate-chip cookies toward him. With her soft blond hair and sweet smile, something about her brought on a calming, the-universe-is-not-such-a-bad-place effect on him.

"No, thanks."

"The kids helped me make them."

"Kylie," he sighed. "I really appreciate all you do for the kids. I realize I haven't been around much." She didn't interrupt him with condolences or reassurances. No, he had already gotten the feeling his nanny believed he spent too much time at work. "My sister was a caring mom. I've been trying to figure out why she was killed. I don't believe it was an accident that Megan hit her head and was found in a lake."

She sat on one of the wooden bar stools and grabbed a cookie. "You've mentioned that you were looking into her case before. Do you think what happened today is connected to her death?"

"Unless that man was your enemy, it has to be. But why try to abduct the kids?"

"I don't know." Kylie flinched and popped the cookie in her mouth. "Did your sister know Hal Alcott?"

"Hal? As in Alcott Real Estate? Megan's husband worked for the company." At her nod, he tried to read her face, but he couldn't tell what she was thinking. "Ev-

eryone around here knows of Hal Alcott. He was at one
of the fund-raising events we had for my cousin's cancer
benefit, but I don't think Megan knew him personally
or hauled two babies into a quiet real-estate office on a
regular basis. Why?"

"Just curious. I'm sorry I brought him up."

He narrowed his gaze. "Are you implying Hal had
something to do with Megan's death?"

"I wasn't implying anything." She sighed. "I remember he'd been brought up on... Never mind."

"What? Brought up on racketeering and money laundering?" At her nod, he said, "Then you should know
all charges were dropped."

She opened her mouth, then clamped it shut and
shook her head.

"Hal is good man. Yes, Tommy worked for him, and
Alcott made the news with the charges, but that doesn't
mean he had anything to do with Megan's death." Luke
managed to control his voice because he knew what it
must look like to an outsider. Even though Hal had been
an acquaintance of his father's for years, Luke had personally conducted a general search into Tommy's work
connections, including Alcott, after his sister's murder.
Kylie was a nanny and he didn't expect to her to understand. She was just trying to help.

He decided to change the subject. "The kids are taken
with you. They're too much for my parents right now."
Luke hadn't spoken to his folks in several weeks. He
had no intention of sharing how, after forty-two years,
he'd learned Sam Dryden wasn't his father. Luke had
idolized and loved the man, but his parents had deceived
him his whole life.

"I love kids." She put the rest of the cookies on the

plate. "Sorry. Stress eating. I'd like to go home early if it's okay. I know the sergeant said he might drop by later. Can I go if I promise to answer my phone?"

"I'm sure Jamison wouldn't mind, but I'll text him to be sure."

He would've preferred her to stay, but he didn't blame her. His parents lived forty minutes away and his only neighbor was a single twenty-five-year-old guy that liked to drink and throw parties a couple of nights a week. Hence, the reason for a nanny. Kylie had already stayed late several times this month. It made it so much easier to have help with the kids. "Go ahead. I've got this."

She stood. "Are you certain?"

"Yes."

"Call me if you need anything. I took meat loaf out of the freezer." She indicated the glass dish on the counter. "I'll put it in the oven and set the timer."

"Thanks." Luke stared after Kylie as she walked out the door. What would he do without her? The memory of her fighting off the attacker at the zoo and then her witnessing the same man being shot in the store parking lot flashed through his mind, making his gut tighten. He was fortunate she hadn't quit today. One thing was certain. If there were any more threats, he'd probably find himself without Kylie as his nanny. And he just wasn't ready for that.

Kylie checked her rearview mirror after she pulled out of Luke's drive. Her nerves were still on edge after Sergeant Jamison questioned her. Had he recognized her? He stared at her, but that was normal when someone was speaking to you. After the explosion that killed the Coffey family, Kylie had hidden out for days before creating a new identity and seeking medical attention. She had been tempted to go to her boss, the assistant director of the US Marshals, and tell him what had really happened that cold morning she had survived Hal's attack. That she had witnessed Hal look over his own handiwork as she lay clinging to life half buried in the debris. But how had someone found her witness? Surely there wasn't a mole in the Marshals. But Hal had money and was a powerful man. Someone must've tipped him off. But who? The thought of a coworker betraying the department was unfathomable. Confused and scared, she had decided to go rogue undercover until she could learn more.

Being a Deputy US Marshal had taught her how easy it was to create a new identity. Without any inside help, though, and new procedures that made it increasingly difficult to pass false documents, Kylie had been forced to claim an unused identity she had in her files that had been created for a witness months prior to the explosion. Her back still bore the scars from the heinous act that should've taken her life. After months of physical therapy, and with the use of hair dye and colored contacts, she went from a brown-eyed brunette with a pixie cut, to a blue-eyed ash-blonde with a blowout style. The longer length and swept bangs sometimes got in the way, but definitely helped conceal more of her features.

A vehicle appeared in her rearview mirror but was too far back to identify what model.

Her tiny RV was only a few miles from Luke's place. Having to move often, the camper was simply more convenient and fit in her limited budget. If she had to relocate, she could do so quickly without breaking any long-term lease or having to put down hefty deposits.

A check in her mirror again showed the vehicle behind her was an emerald-green minivan.

She kept her eye on the vehicle even though it didn't appear to be a threat, but she circled the block just to be sure. The van kept going straight on the highway.

Finally, she pulled into Wildwood RV Park and drove to the last lane, where her camper was. She had also rented the space next to hers so some bulky, long motor home wouldn't move in and block her view of the rest of the park. As she stepped out of the Jeep, the sounds of explosions and gunfire blared from a nearby television. On the other side of the park, a dog yapped. Everything else was quiet.

Grabbing her Glock, keys and purse, she walked up the stone pathway. The ceramic frog she'd put in front of the glass door was still in place. She went inside and continued her normal routine of putting her purse on the counter, and with her cell and Glock in hand, proceeded to check out the small trailer. Nothing had been disturbed.

She set her weapon on the kitchen counter, clicked on the television and flipped to a local news station. The national evening news was airing, and the local news would come on in thirty-five minutes. That didn't give her much time. She quickly changed into jogging shorts and headed to the small exercise room in the clubhouse. Two older-model treadmills faced a huge glass wall that allowed a fantastic view of the front entrance to the park. She stepped on the closest machine and warmed up for only a minute before she turned it up. In no time, she was running at a fast pace.

Stress did two things to her—made her hungry for something sweet and eager to work out.

Thirteen minutes later, she had run two miles and was dripping with sweat. Her pulse raced, and she had to catch her breath before chugging some water. As she threw the paper cup into the trash, she noticed a red Dodge Charger pull into the park. Standing to the side of the window, she watched the vehicle ease down the rock drive to her street. Tinted windows kept her from seeing if a man or woman drove the car. The Charger stopped, but then a few seconds later continued on.

Keeping an eye on the vehicle as it exited the park, she hurried back to her camper and performed another walk-through before making a turkey-and-cheese sandwich. She grabbed a bottle of water, hit Record on the television in case she wanted to view the coverage later and settled in her recliner just as the news came on. A video of police cars at the dollar store flashed across the screen. Of course, it would be the top news story. A young, pretty reporter by the name of Elizabeth Anne looked pleased to be on the segment. She pointed to the Tahoe surrounded by yellow tape while narrating the account, and then the camera cut to the sergeant in front of her Jeep. At first, all the view showed was the back end of the car, but as the camera zoomed in, there was Kylie hurrying around her vehicle to the driver's side.

Shock held her in place, as she was too stunned to breathe. No, this couldn't have happened. She slammed her hand on the side of the recliner.

Kylie had been careful for three years. Three years! She'd even taken it so seriously that when people were taking pictures on their cell phones—which was all the time—she would turn or hurry out of the way. She didn't want to risk showing up on someone's social-media page and have a stranger—or worse, someone from her past—recognize her.

What if Hal, or one of his men, saw her?

Would they come after her? Her family?

Rewinding the news segment, she watched the shot again. And again. No, she didn't think the view was clear enough for anyone to recognize her. She had kept her head down, and the only time the camera captured her face was as she went around the back of the bumper.

She turned down the volume and put her dishes in the sink. As she was turning to go to her bedroom, something flashed across her window. She glanced out the blinds. The red Charger cruised by again.

The sun was setting, and it would be dark soon. The car's headlights weren't on. It could be one of her neighbors, but her instincts told her no.

She startled at the vibrating of her cell phone. As she continued to watch out the window, she glanced at the caller ID. Luke's number. "Hello."

"Kylie, I wanted to let you know Sergeant Jamison is coming over in a bit to ask you more questions. I gave him as many answers as I could. It's not uncommon for police to ask several rounds of questions."

She understood investigative work but didn't say so. Rocky Creek was a couple of hours from Dallas where Hal was indicted, and the Rocky Creek PD would've had nothing to do with his investigation. There would be no reason the sergeant would recognize her any more than Luke would. But every occasion she spent time with anyone, law enforcement or not, she was taking a chance.

Should she tell Luke someone was driving around

her place? What if a potential camper was checking out the park searching for a good spot? Moving to the other side of her RV, she looked out the west window. Dark pink from the setting sun silhouetted a small grove of pecan trees, but the road couldn't be seen from here. Neither could the car.

"Do we need to come over? I don't mind."

"Please, keep the kids at home. Unless…"

"Unless what?"

She returned to the front window and movement caught her eye. A man with something clutched in his hands hunched down and disappeared behind her Jeep. The muscles in Kylie's neck twitched. Justice. Integrity. Service. The US Marshals Service motto played through her mind just like when Assistant Director Seth Wheeler used to quote it before their team faced a threatening showdown. She retrieved her gun and made certain a bullet was in the chamber. Careful to stand to the side so that she wasn't an easy target, she said, "Luke, somebody's here. I don't know—"

A bright orange ball flashed. Before she could react, the window shattered, showering her with glass. Tiny shards stabbed her. Flames landed on her recliner and erupted into a massive fireball.

Get out. All she could think was that she needed to get out.

THREE

"Kylie?" Fear gripped Luke as the line went dead. He ran back to the kids' room. They were stirring from their naps, and he scooped them up. The thought of taking the twins with him made him uncomfortable, but what choice did he have? If he had anyone nearby, he'd ask them to watch the kids, but there was no one. Hence, the reason he'd hired Kylie.

Zoe's lip puckered as she began to cry.

"It's okay, sweetheart. Uncle Luke is taking you for a ride." He turned off the oven with the meat loaf still inside and grabbed a handful of cookies and the diaper bags on his way out the door. He gave each child a treat and then hit Kylie's name on his Bluetooth as he sped out of the drive.

No answer. The pit in his stomach grew taut, his nerves on edge. He hit another number.

Jax picked up on the third ring. "O'Neill."

"I need you to meet me at Kylie's." Luke rattled off the address of the RV park.

"I'm almost to Rocky Creek now. What happened?"

"We were on the phone and she had just told me somebody was at her house. I heard a crash and the line went dead. She won't answer now. En route to her place."

"Dryden, why would someone target your nanny? Why was the man who botched abducting your kids murdered in broad daylight?"

"I have no idea, but I'm going to find out. I'm pulling into the RV park."

"Five minutes behind you."

An orange glow came from the back of the park and Luke knew it had to be Kylie's place. He held his breath as he sped down the lane and then slammed on his brakes as close to her camper as he dared while still being able to keep an eye on the kids. Adrenaline pumped from a mixture of fear for Kylie and anger at whoever had targeted her. Flames raged from the window, creating a huge mushroom cloud of smoke. As he opened the truck door, heat slammed into him. Zoe and Braden gawked at the fire from the safety of their car seats, and Luke handed them each another cookie. "I'll be right back."

Since he had keyless entry, he left the truck running, locked the doors and ran toward the burning inferno, keeping a lookout for the perpetrator.

"Over here." A man with white hair who sported a Hawaiian shirt and khaki shorts waved him over. "She needs help."

Relief flooded him when he spotted Kylie sitting on the ground in the empty lot across from the burning trailer.

"I'm fine. Let go of me." She struggled to stand, but the man kept trying to push her back down.

"I've got this." He flashed his badge at the elderly man. "Texas Ranger."

"Oh." The man backed away a few steps but didn't leave.

Luke leaned over her. "Did you see who did this? Is he still here?"

Kylie's shoulders stiffened, and she shook her head. "He was driving a red Dodge Charger. He had split by the time I made it out of my house."

"Are you injured?"

"A few cuts and maybe singed a bit." She stood and twisted her arm to show him and was visibly shaking, although she tried to hide it. "Stings right there but nothing serious. He shot fire through my window. Probably a Molotov cocktail, although I'm not sure. Where are the twins?"

"In my truck." His gaze narrowed. "How do you know about Molotov cocktails?"

She swatted the air. "I watch a lot of drama shows. Let's get out of here. I don't trust him not to come back."

"I agree." He needed to get her and the kids to safety before he could concentrate on finding the man who did this. Kylie stood straight and appeared composed, but he had detected the slight tremor in her voice. "Come with me."

As they reached his truck, Jax pulled up and Luke waited while Kylie climbed in. "O'Neill, this is Kylie Stone. I'm getting her and the kids out of here." He relayed the description of the car and let Kylie explain what happened. "I'm taking them to my parents' house. Call me with any questions or if you have any news."

"That's a good idea. I'll finish up here."

"Sergeant Jamison should be here soon because he was supposed to interview Kylie. Tell him I'll give him a call."

At Jax's nod, Luke pulled onto the street in the direction of the main highway.

"Will your parents be okay with me staying the night? I can rent a room at a hotel. I don't mind."

"I'd rather you stay with us. Mom's knee has been giving her trouble. I've told her she needed to get it fixed, but she claims to have too many things to do. She won't take time off. I'd feel better if you stayed and helped. I'll pay you for your time, of course."

Kylie stared out the window.

A heaviness weighed down on his chest. No telling what she was thinking. These attacks were his fault. He shouldn't have asked Kylie to be his nanny. Even though many in the Rocky Creek Police Department believed Megan's death an accident, he knew it was murder. He'd been on the outs with his parents ever since he'd learned they'd deceived him, but he should've let his folks have the twins until he found Megan's killer. Then Kylie wouldn't be in this mess.

"Are you sure you're okay? Do you need to go to the hospital?"

"Nah. I'd rather get the kids somewhere safe." She sighed and turned her blue eyes on him. "I'm not hurt. Just upset."

"Let me see." He switched on the overhead light and turned her hand over. The skin was red, but not blistered. "There's burn cream in my first-aid kit under the seat."

She found the kit and the cream. He waited until she was through before he turned off the light. "Did you get a good look at the man?"

"No. That's what I was thinking about. Willing my brain to recall any details that would help identify the man."

"Had you seen the car before?"

"No."

"You're certain this wasn't the same vehicle as the man in the ski mask at the store?"

Lines formed across her forehead. "Different car. The man at the store drove a sedan. This was a red Dodge Charger."

Luke looked at her. Her hair was falling in her face. "Think about this guy at your trailer. Any information would help. Was he big? Tall? Young?"

"I don't know." Her shoulders slumped. "It was getting dark and his windows were tinted. I saw him hunched down, not standing, behind my Jeep. I just don't know."

"Hun-gee," Braden yelled from the back seat.

Kylie turned around in her seat. "Oh, no. Have you not eaten supper?"

"Afraid not," Luke said. "They were just waking up from their nap when I called you about Jamison coming over. Which reminds me. I need to talk with the sergeant."

He called Jamison, but Jax had already filled him in. It was always a relief when local authorities worked well with their agency.

After he hung up, Kylie asked, "So the kids didn't get any meat loaf?"

"No, but I did remember to turn off the oven so it wouldn't burn."

"Well, at least that's something." She smiled. "Have they been changed?"

"No. I was in a hurry to leave. I'm not very good with kids." What was he thinking? Of course the twins would need changing. He'd simply received Kylie's call and hurried out of the house.

"Nonsense. You haven't had much practice. Did you remember their diaper bags?"

"In the back seat. And I also gave them cookies."

She laughed, a beautiful sound. Kylie had a way of not tossing blame, which made him feel even worse. "I'm sure they didn't mind that. How far to your parents?"

"About forty minutes. Maybe thirty minutes from here."

"Good. Pull over at the next convenience store and I'll change the kids. You can get them some milk and see if they have any fresh fruit, like an apple or banana, to tide them over."

Why was it that he was a Texas Ranger and she the babysitter, but it felt like he was the one leaning on her for support?

Kylie changed the kids and had them back in their seats by the time Luke returned to the truck. He had not only bought milk, sliced apples and a banana, but also a container of yogurt, cheese crackers and a cup of grapes. "You loaded up."

He nodded and shot her a smile, a dimple forming on his right cheek. "I know. Don't know if Mom has any snacks for the kids so I thought it would be good to have extras."

"Great idea." She twisted around in the seat and handed each of the kids a slice of apple. "Not too much."

Zoe took her slice and then nibbled while Braden crammed the whole thing in his mouth. After he chomped his, Kylie broke a slice in half and gave him only a little at a time. Taking care of the twins helped keep her mind off of having a flaming bottle bomb shot into her house. Perhaps that wasn't such a good thing. She needed to think about how close she'd come to being killed. Plan on how to prevent becoming a target again.

The questions that plagued her were who and why. Maybe the big guy at the zoo had wanted her instead of the twins? Maybe the kids weren't in any danger except when they were near her. That was a sobering thought.

Had her identity been compromised? If so, Hal Alcott must be behind the attack. Since she'd placed him at the scene of the Coffey family's deaths, he couldn't afford for her to talk.

Everyone believed she was dead. If someone knew she was really Melody Garner, what did they have to lose by killing her for real? She shivered.

"You all right?"

She looked at Luke and found concerned eyes staring back.

His eyebrows arched. "The kids have been hollering for more."

"Oh, I'm sorry." She handed both the kids another slice of apple.

Luke directed his gaze back to the road, a frown firmly in place. "I shouldn't have hired you as a nanny. Or anyone to watch the kids. This is my fault. I should've known I could put you in danger."

"What? No." She wanted to tell Luke the truth. Tell him everything. Not having anyone—no family, co-workers, a significant other or anyone—was excruciating. Never again would she take family and close friends for granted. The only thing good that had come out of the last three years of totally being alone was that she found herself talking to God more often. "We don't even know who's targeting us. Or if someone is after the kids or just me."

He gripped the steering wheel tighter. "I appreciate you saying so, but I doubt anyone would be after you unless it has to do with you working for me. Why would anyone want to hurt you?"

She looked out the window. How could she answer? If she told him the truth, would he tell Jax O'Neill and the rest of the Rangers? How long until everyone knew she was alive? Was she ready to take the chance? "Luke, I don't know who was at my camper tonight. When we find out who, maybe we'll know why."

He didn't respond but looked deep in thought.

The highway turned into a paved road, the headlights illuminating white vinyl fences. Big homes with lots of acreage lined both sides of the road. A mile or so farther, he pulled through a large piped gate, with Dryden Farms above the entry. The drive wound around a large pasture for a half mile before coming to an old two-story farmhouse. Unlike the neighbors, who had newer houses, this one was outfitted with barns and painted wooden fences. Kylie sucked in her breath.

Home. This place could be on the cover of a magazine. Even though it was a bit larger, the estate reminded her of her parents' house. The sudden ache for family squeezed her throat. Kylie could go for days without letting the worry for the people she'd left behind overtake her. Then something like the sight of Luke's parents' house would knock her off balance, and the emotions and guilt came flooding back. The birthdays and holidays she'd missed. The birth of her younger sister's first child. Her brother's high-school graduation. And, especially, not being there when her mother learned she had cancer.

Her mother's surgery, risky at best, was scheduled for two weeks from tomorrow. Kylie kept up with everyone because Emma, her youngest sister, just seventeen, posted everything on Facebook. If Kylie ever got back home, she needed to remind Emma about internet safety and privacy settings, but for now, she was grateful for the connection to her past.

"Well, this is it." Luke turned to her. "I'll get the kids."

"I'll help you." Kylie got out and went to get Zoe.

"Oh-h-h. You're here." A pretty lady with a classy layered bob hurried down the wooden steps of the huge front porch and headed their way. "Let Grandma see those babies." She went to Kylie's side of the truck, and Kylie stepped out of the way.

"Zoe. You're getting so big!" The little girl looked unsure as her grandma unstrapped her from the seat and pulled her into a hug. "Look at you. You're the prettiest girl ever."

Her grandma put Zoe on her hip and hurried with a slight limp to the other side of the truck, but Luke already had Braden out and was waiting on Kylie. The woman's smile faltered. "Thank you for bringing them by, Luke. We really appreciate it."

"I appreciate you putting us up on such short notice. Mom, this is Kylie Stone, the twins' nanny. Kylie, this is my mom, Dottie."

Dottie gave her a warm smile. "Glad to meet you, Kylie. Excuse my manners—come on in, dear."

Kylie carried the diaper bags and snacks and followed them into the house. A big open room with white shiplap and leather furniture greeted her. Either someone was burning a candle, or his mother had been baking.

Dottie brushed Braden's cheek. "He has gotten so big."

Luke sighed. "He's only a few months older, Mom."

"I know that, son, but I've missed them."

"I should've brought them by."

"You sure should have." A tall man with a touch of gray hair strode into the room. His broad shoulders told Kylie that he either worked out or worked hard to stay in shape. Seeing the beautiful farm, probably the latter.

"Grandpa!" Braden held out his hands.

"I've been busy." Luke set Braden on the floor and wiped his hands on his jeans.

Luke's dad picked up the boy and tossed him in the air. "Hello, biggin. How's Grandpa's little helper?"

The toddler grinned and yelled, "Tractor."

The older man laughed. "It's too dark now, but I can take you in the morning."

Luke cleared his throat. "Da—uh, I told you I'd rather the kids stay inside until we know what's going on."

"Nonsense," his dad huffed. "No one's going to mess with these kids while I'm around. I may've only been a state trooper, but I know how to defend my family."

"You know—" Luke cut himself off and gave his dad a glassy stare. Finally, he let out a heavy sigh. "Kylie, this is my dad, Sam Dryden."

"Glad to meet you, sir." She smiled. "You have a beautiful place."

Sam grumbled, "Thanks."

The tension in the room hung thick, like a stormy night. Kylie turned to Dottie and asked, "Where would you like their things?"

Luke's mom reached out and touched her hand. "Come with me."

With the diaper bags in tow, Kylie followed her to a back room that contained two cribs, one decorated with tractors and the other with unicorns. She wouldn't have thought the scheme would've meshed, but the perfect highlights of yellow and green matched each twin's personality to a T.

"You can put their bags on the changing table."

"I'm sorry, but Luke had to leave in a hurry and didn't have time to pack clothes. I'm afraid all they have is the extra set in the bag."

Dottie waved her hand. "Not to worry. We have plenty of baby things here." She dug through a drawer and pulled out two sets of pajamas.

Curiosity made Kylie want to ask about the seemingly strained relationship between Luke and his parents, but she refrained. It wasn't uncommon for families to have problems. His parents' reactions to the twins told her they loved and missed their grandchildren. Had Luke purposely kept them away after Megan had died? If so, why?

"I'll bathe the kids in this bathroom. Feel free to use our guest bath down the hall."

Kylie smiled. She hadn't looked in a mirror, but she could guess what she must look like. With the fire, she hadn't exactly had time to pack a bag. "Thanks."

As if she had read her mind, Dottie said, "If you need any clothes, there's some in that bedroom." She pointed to the adjoining room. "Make yourself at home."

She thanked her, went into the room and turned on the light. A beautiful blue iron antique bed covered with a yellow-and-denim-blue quilt was the focal point.

Sheer white curtains hung over the huge window and white shiplap covered the walls. Stuffed animals and a little girl's jewelry box sat on a distressed dresser. This must've been Megan's room.

Sadness seeped into her bones. To lose a life at such a young age had to be almost unbearable on her family. Instantly, her mind again went to her own family in Wichita Falls. Even though she was alive, her mom and siblings had gone through the same grief. Kylie closed her eyes against the pain. She wanted to go home and let them know she hadn't died in that explosion.

Very soon her family would learn the truth. Hal Alcott would be brought to justice. Then she would come out of hiding.

She found T-shirts, shorts and cotton pajama pants in the drawers. A quick look in the closet showed her jeans and some dressier clothes. Even though the items must've been several years old, Kylie found plenty of things that never went out of style. When she had searched Megan on the internet, Kylie had learned she had married Tommy Doane almost three years ago and had lived on her own since she was twenty. Kylie grabbed a Texas A&M T-shirt and a pair of cotton shorts, and went to take a quick shower.

After finishing, she almost felt normal. As she dried herself off, cabinet doors slamming and the low hum of people talking told her Luke's family was busy. She went back to Megan's room and closed the door. Her laptop had surely burned up in the camper, so she pulled out her phone. She'd have to dig out her iPad, which had all of her files, from the Jeep later. Her laptop was much easier to use for reading, and she'd have to buy a new one later. She pulled up her sister's Facebook page. She scrolled down—several new pictures had been posted. One of Emma and her best friend. A selfie with Emma and the family dog, Nash, who was perked up and watching television. A glimpse of her brother and Mom standing in the kitchen, too far away to get a good look, but she could imagine the conversation.

A smile crept up her lips. They all looked so *normal*. Everyday life of coming and going, and then spending time with one another. Something Kylie now realized she'd taken for granted. The next photo was simply a map of the diner in town that they loved to eat at. Sara's Diner. Kylie's chest grew heavy as she scrolled through the pictures and browsed the silly comments left by others.

A post left on Sunday contained only words, no pics. *Please pray for my mom. She's running a fever and they won't be able to operate in two weeks unless it comes down.*

Unbidden tears blurred her vision. Maybe she should show up at her mom's house. Instruct her family to tell no one she was alive.

Even as the thought teased her longing to go home, Kylie knew she couldn't do it. Hal's men always used family and friends to threaten his victims. She couldn't take the chance. Time was running out. She had to see Hal brought to justice.

FOUR

Kylie turned off her cell phone and checked the mirror to see if her face was red. A little blotchy, so she dug through the drawers and found a compact of face powder.

When she marched back into the living room, Zoe and Braden sat in their grandpa's lap listening to him read *The Three Little Pigs*. She almost laughed as he exaggerated the *huff* and *puff* sounds.

Braden looked up at her and grinned, pure joy in his expression. "Grandpa's reading to me."

"I see that." She glanced at Zoe, who seemed content to be reading with her grandpa and brother.

Luke stood in the kitchen alone, a large glass of iced tea in front of him, his expression solemn. "Would you like something to drink? Tea, water or lemonade."

"Lemonade sounds great." After he set down the glass, she whispered, "Has she always been this quiet?"

He looked over at his dad, who had begun reading again. "Zoe?" At her nod, he said, "Not this quiet."

"I found it." Dottie whisked into the room holding a movie. Sam didn't look up but kept reading as his wife made for the entertainment center. "I hope they haven't seen this yet. I'll make ice-cream floats in a bit."

"Zoe sure looks like Megan, doesn't she?" Sam boasted.

Dottie hollered back, "I thought the same thing."

Kylie's breath hitched. The pain of losing a daughter must be unbearable, she thought, especially seeing the resemblance in her babies.

His mother continued, "Braden has your chin."

"You think so?" Sam chuckled.

Luke jerked his head, indicating the French doors off the living room. His face was beet red. "Come on. Let's talk."

Kylie couldn't help but smile at his parents' excitement in entertaining the twins as she followed Luke out the door, drink in hand, to the large deck. What was wrong with Luke? She sat in the wicker chair with the bold yellow and pink throw pillows. He sat across from her on the large white wooden porch swing. Even though the furniture was large and sturdy, the Ranger looked like a misfit in the cottage-looking setting.

Luke continued the conversation started in the kitchen. "Braden has always been more rambunctious than his sister, but she's grown clingier and more subdued since Megan's death."

She nodded. "I'm sorry." Any more response seemed inadequate, so she left the comment at that. Luke's worry lines had increased, and she didn't want to pile more on his shoulders. Kylie wanted to help the toddlers, but she also was aware that she wouldn't be a part of their life for long. Was it fair to let Zoe grow attached and then leave? No. Her heart was pulled in two different directions, but she had to do what was best for the children. That would be to encourage Luke and his parents to be the ones the kids leaned on.

"I appreciate you coming over to help with the kids. I know it's asking a lot."

"I don't mind. They're sweethearts." She sipped her drink.

He stared at her for a moment. "Do you have family nearby?"

She swallowed, almost choking on her lemonade. She coughed to clear her throat. She wasn't expecting the sudden change of topic. How did she answer? As Kylie Stone? Or as Melody Garner with a large family? Normally, she gave the standard I-don't-have-family-close-to-me answer. "I haven't seen them in a while."

He continued to watch her, like he was weighing her words. "You're good with kids."

"Thank you." Time to move past her involvement, but she had to be careful. "Your parents seem excited to see them."

"I suppose." His expression lost its softness.

She wasn't going to let his sudden change in mood stop her. Again, she'd never be anything to the kids except a temporary sitter. She had plans to go back to her family. "Do you trust your parents to care for them?"

"Kylie, like I said, I appreciate your help. But I don't want to discuss my parents."

"I like them. Family is precious. You never…" She wanted to say that you never knew how important relatives were until you lost them, but he'd lost Megan, so she kept the words to herself.

"Like I said, not going there."

The look he gave her probably intimidated a lot of people. Coworkers. Criminals. But Kylie had known tough law-enforcement officers, and she realized many times that a tough exterior was brought on by something painful deep inside. "Fine. But I wasn't worried about you. It's the kids. Zoe and Braden. Their life has been turned upside down. They need you. All of you."

Pain flashed across his face before he looked toward the yard. A breeze blew and a sudden chill bit her. She rubbed her arms.

"Sorry. I won't mention it again. Not my place." The sooner this case was over, the better for everyone. She didn't know why she was involving herself in his family, anyway. She needed Hal Alcott behind bars. Then she could go back to being Melody and forget the fictional life of Kylie she'd created. "Have you heard back from Jax?"

"We've talked."

"Any idea who burned my camper?"

"Not yet. The firefighters put out the flames, but it doesn't look like much is salvageable from your home. Thankfully, no other trailers caught fire. Your Jeep will need to be deep cleaned from all the smoke, the paint is blistered and Jax said something about the tires needing to be replaced. And we don't know if that's the extent of the damage. Will be tomorrow at the earliest before we learn what kind of explosive he used." He crossed his arms. "I'm struggling with the why."

"Me, too. Makes me wonder if my attacker at the zoo was after the kids or not. Whatever his intentions were, I want to find out soon."

"Exactly. Get some sleep." He unfolded his arms and leaned closer. "Will you be all right here with my parents and the twins tomorrow?"

She'd been thinking about that. "What if I'm the only

target? Wouldn't that put your parents and the kids in danger? I think your folks can handle them without my help."

He shoved his hand through his hair. "I'll let you know in the morning."

It sounded like she'd been dismissed. She stood to go into the house, but she couldn't leave without setting the record straight. "Luke, I know I'm just the nanny, but I do care about Zoe and Braden, and I want what's best for them."

As she started to go into the house, she heard his response. "Me, too, Kylie."

The next morning, brown eyes connected with Kylie's. She recognized the reserved excitement in the Ranger's stoic demeanor.

He clicked off his cell. "I just got a lead on Tommy Doane, Megan's missing husband."

Kylie already knew who Tommy was and that he had disappeared two months before Megan's death, but she remained silent.

"I need to check this out. I'll be back in a little while." He headed toward the front door.

"No. Wait up." She heard him sigh. When he turned, she continued, "I'm going with you."

"No way. You'll be safer with my folks. I need you to help with the twins. And Tommy has nothing to do with you."

"Luke Dryden, your parents are perfectly capable at tending to the kids, especially since your dad used to be in law enforcement. You might not believe this, but I may be of more assistance than you realize. I've read about your sister's case. I'd like to help."

"Reading about a case doesn't mean you're in the know. I can't take an innocent civilian along."

"Seriously? I fought off a kidnapper, witnessed him being shot and then survived someone burning my trailer all *without* you by my side. I can't possibly be in any more danger riding along than being at the house. If your sister's husband has anything to do with these attacks, I have a right to know."

Luke glanced at the clock on the wall and then scrutinized her, his eyes taking her in. She couldn't tell what his conclusions were where she was concerned, but he finally said, "All right."

The two words sounded more like an ultimatum.

She hurried to climb into the truck. They had no more pulled out of the gate before she asked, "What did you learn about Tommy?"

He stared straight ahead. "Don't you think it's you who needs to be the one explaining? What do you know about my sister's death?"

Time to come clean, at least partly, with what she knew about Megan. "I know she was found in a quarry. The authorities ruled her death an accident, but it didn't make sense she would be out there by herself. Her husband had been gone for two months before her death and no one seems to know where he is. His disappearance throws up a major red flag. Sounds like he may also be dead."

Luke worked his jaw as he turned onto the main highway. "You listening to gossip or did my mother tell you this?"

"Oh, no, your parents haven't said anything."

"Last night was the first time you've met them? Or have they been to my house?" His hand gripped the steering wheel. "It's important you're honest with me."

Honest. She'd come to hate that word. How can you be undercover and honest at the same time? "Your parents have never been to your house while I've been there. I didn't meet them until last night. Neither your mom nor dad have said anything about your sister last night or any other time. That's the truth."

He released a breath, his grip relaxing.

"I don't know what is going on with your family, but I assure you, I haven't been talking with your folks. Can you tell me what's going on?" Okay, guilt hovered. Here she was, asking him to be open, but she still hadn't come clean with him. She had to be certain he wouldn't blow her cover, and that Hal was really the one behind the attacks. Once she revealed her identity, there was no taking it back. Seth Wheeler, her boss at the US Marshals Service, used to say, "You're the only one you can trust to keep a secret. Once you share information, it's all out of your hands." Specifically, he was referring to those in WITSEC, but it was true for rogue undercover agents, too.

Luke glanced her way for a second, then turned his attention back to the road. "A call came into the Rocky Creek PD. A neighbor reported seeing someone going in and out of Tommy and Megan's house. Their property is in probate until it's determined whether Tommy will return to claim the place. No one has been in the house for weeks, and it caught the attention of the neighbor, Mrs. Bryant."

Kylie glanced at him out the corner of her eye. Lines were etched across his forehead. When she had first read of Megan's death, she believed there might be a connection to Hal Alcott because he's been known to hurt family members to pressure people to do what he wanted. Lori Coffey's husband had worked for Hal, and he'd shared with Lori their illegal activities. The husband had even told many of the names of the men involved.

Tommy Doane was on that list.

Since Tommy had disappeared, it only made sense he may have crossed Hal.

Kylie had hoped to learn of the connection Tommy had to Hal, but after working for Luke for two months, she still hadn't found anything, from either the tight-lipped Ranger or paperwork in his house. She knew it had been a long shot but had still hoped.

They drove to the west side of town to a newer neighborhood. The two-story brick and stone houses had well-manicured lawns with plenty of flowers, bringing out the pretty Texas colors. Bricked mailboxes lined the concrete road. A tanned, athletic lady jogged on the sidewalk pushing a stroller, earbuds dangling onto her shoulders.

Kylie had driven by this house numerous times in the past few months. She had never been inside even though she was confident in her ability to pick locks. She didn't need some neighbor to call in a suspicious person and then take the chance of the police showing up and recognizing her.

Keeping her identity secret ruled her life.

Luke pulled his truck to a cul-de-sac and into the drive of the beautiful stone home trimmed in cedar.

"Nice house."

He glanced at her but didn't comment as he grabbed his hat.

"What kind of vehicle does Tommy drive?"

"The last we heard it was a red Corvette Z06 convertible, but there's nothing to say he hasn't switched vehicles. He loves his cars."

Whew. Definitely out of her price range. She grabbed the handle to open her door.

"You coming in?" he asked, as if he disagreed with her decision.

"Sure am. I didn't ride all this way to sit in the truck. I may notice something in the house you don't."

"I'm not planning on staying long. I've searched the house numerous times. I want to see if anyone's been here."

"Good. Then it shouldn't be a problem if I join you." She followed him up the concrete drive and watched while he punched in the code to the garage door. They waited as it rolled up, but then found the garage empty. "Where's Megan's car?"

His eyes narrowed. "It's in my parents' barn."

Okay. No need to expound on that. Kylie remembered when they lost her dad almost seven years ago. It had taken three years before her mom would even go through his clothes. Many of Dad's things were still in his shop, or in her parents' bedroom, waiting for him like he could walk through the door at any moment. Kylie tried not to think that her family had probably gone through the same thing with her "death."

They entered the house through a sort of mudroom-laundry room. The area was almost as big as her entire camper. Next was the kitchen, with a huge island and granite countertops. One of those large commercial freezer-refrigerator combinations almost took up a whole wall.

While Luke disappeared to the back of the house, Kylie opened the trash compactor. No trash, not even a bag. She checked the refrigerator and found normal staple items such as jelly, sauces and butter. No milk or anything that would spoil. From the looks of the kitchen, no one had prepared or eaten food there since Megan's death. If they had, they must have taken out the trash with them.

Luke walked back into the room. "There's no sign anyone has been here."

Kylie did another quick survey of the kitchen. Keys hung by the door. Everything was clean, almost giving the impression that a housekeeper had been there. No visible dust. "Did Megan use any kind of cleaning service?"

Luke thought for a moment. "I think so. I remember Tommy complaining that even with a maid, Megan still struggled to keep the house picked up."

She rolled her eyes. "I'm sure she did with twins. There's no trash in here. You think we should check the outside receptacle?"

"Good idea. Be right back."

As soon as Luke shut the door, Kylie went to the master bedroom and peered in the nightstand. Nothing but a couple of FBI thriller books and things like toenail clippers and hand lotion. No weapons or mysterious notes. One could always hope. The dresser drawers contained nothing helpful. All but two of the ten drawers appeared to belong to Megan, and the other two held men's underwear and socks all lined in perfect rows. Did Megan fold her husband's clothes or was he so tidy he did his own laundry?

Not that it mattered—Kylie's brothers couldn't care less about things like that.

"Find anything?"

She jumped at Luke's voice. "No. Just trying to get a feel for who your sister and brother-in-law were."

Luke's brown eyes dimmed. "Did you learn anything?"

She shut the drawers. "Not really. Was Tommy a neat fanatic?"

"I suppose." He shrugged. "He complained about everything. Megan was never good enough."

"I'm sorry. That must've been hard for a big brother."

"There was nothing in the trash bins. No evidence of a break-in or anyone being here. If someone came in, he or she took what they wanted and left."

Kylie noticed he didn't respond to the big-brother comment. Her heart went out to him. No doubt guilt for losing someone he wanted to protect was one thing Luke and she had in common.

When they walked back through the living room, a collage of photos on a table caught her eye. There were several of the twins, including a couple with Megan. Kylie had already searched online for the news report of Megan's death and on social-media pages. When Kylie searched the internet, she'd learned Megan was on Facebook and Instagram. Again, no pictures of Tommy, and he wasn't on social media. "No pictures of Tommy?"

Luke came and looked over her shoulder. "I never paid much attention. I do think she had their wedding photos at one time. She had a sixteen-by-twenty photo of her in her gown above the mantel."

A copper-and-pewter star wall decoration stood above the cedar mantel now.

"Is there a picture missing from here?" Kylie pointed to the wall. Four pictures but something seemed off.

And by looking around, everything, including decorations, seemed planned out.

"Maybe."

"Would Tommy have taken it?"

"Or maybe it fell and broke, and Megan never had time to replace it."

"True." She nodded.

"I've seen enough." Luke headed for the door, his expression grim.

Kylie's throat ached. She couldn't imagine losing one of her siblings to murder. "I'd like to look at the kids' room if that's okay."

He stopped his progression to the door and sighed. "I don't know what you're hoping to find, but it's fine by me."

She knew walking through his sister's home, where she'd lived with her two babies, must be painful for him. But at least he hadn't argued. Some people were contrary for the sake of being contrary. Luke wasn't like that, and she was relieved. At the back of the house, she found the room decorated in giraffes and monkeys. Two cribs were against the wall. A baby monitor sat on the dresser. A zoo-cage toy box overflowed with toys, some spilling onto the floor. Again, it was as if no one had picked up or moved a thing since Megan's death.

"Luke." She looked at him as he stood in the doorway. "You have two cribs at your house—why didn't you take the ones from here?"

"I didn't know if Tommy would come back to his house."

"Do you think he will?"

"No. Even if he did, I'd probably fight him for the kids. Child abandonment."

She figured as much. The Drydens seemed like a protective family. "You think Tommy's dead?"

He nodded. "At first, I thought he'd left my sister because they weren't getting along. But why be gone so long? He should've returned for his things. The house. The kids. He may have been a jerk to Megan, but I think he'd come back for the twins."

Kylie could see that. And this house was too expensive to let it sit unless they owed more than what the home was worth. She could ask Luke more about that later. He'd been open with her, but she didn't want to push it too far.

The closet door stood open, and she peeked in. Toys filled the shelves and clothes hung on racks, with more folded in tubs along the floor. She could imagine how many clothes two kids could go through before the age of two. On the top shelf sat a large LEGO container with the lid askew. She reached for it. Empty. "Where are the LEGO pieces?"

He walked up behind her. "I don't know."

"That's weird." She looked around, picked up the lids on the tubs and looked in the toy box. These weren't the mega size blocks, but the small ones made for older kids. "Just an empty box."

"Maybe Megan put them in the attic or something. If I remember correctly, those plastic pieces can wreak havoc if stepped on barefoot."

She shot him a smile. "You're probably right."

He glanced at his phone. "We really need to go."

She shoved the empty LEGO container back onto the shelf and followed him out the door. While he locked up, she climbed back into the truck. She couldn't help but feel something was off. The neighbor had seen someone, but the house didn't show any signs of being broken into. Her mind kept going back to the empty container.

Of course, it may've been as simple as Luke suggested—that Megan put them somewhere else.

Up the street, a black, jacked-up truck with tinted windows was parked at the curb. The glare was too dark to see inside.

Luke got in and shut the door.

"Do you think the neighbor was mistaken?"

He scrubbed his hand over his face. "I really don't know. Mrs. Bryant lives in the house to the right of Megan's, and she has a great view."

"You could have the house checked for fingerprints."

"The Texas Rangers are working Megan's case. They'll look into it." He put the truck in Reverse and backed out of the drive.

Should she drop the subject? She didn't want to press Luke too hard, but she wanted him to check out Hal more thoroughly. "Tommy worked as a real-estate agent. What was dangerous about that job?"

"Why so many questions?"

As they passed the black truck, Kylie noted a man inside. She turned her attention back to Luke. "I want to help. Don't you think it's strange that Tommy worked for Hal Alcott and Hal was involved in that—"

Luke slammed on the brakes, and Kylie slid forward from the jolt. "What are you doing? Spying on my family? What are you, a nanny who blogs about murders in her spare time?"

Pop. Pop.

The back window of his truck exploded, tiny shards of glass showering them.

A scream escaped her lips as she dove down in the

seat. Instinctively, her hand grasped for her gun at her ankle, but the Glock and the holster weren't there. Her fists tightened. Her weapon was in her Jeep where she put it after the fire because there was no place to conceal it wearing jogging shorts. How was she supposed to bring down this guy or defend herself? She clung to the leather seat, her mind whirling with how to help Luke without giving away her cover.

FIVE

Luke hit the accelerator and shouted, "You hurt?"

"No." Kylie stayed low in the seat as she peeked over the dashboard. "Maybe a nick or two, but mainly the shots startled me."

A glance in his rearview mirror showed the black pickup truck was on his bumper, the roar of his engine deafening with no back glass.

Luke pushed his speed to the max as they flew down the residential street, and he fought the urge to go faster. Being summer, kids were out of school and people were busy outside.

"Watch out," Kylie warned.

A small car puttered in front of him. He swung to the right, narrowly missing a parked convertible, and was forced onto the sidewalk. Another parked car loomed in front of them. He clenched his teeth as he swung back onto the road just in time to miss the car.

Pop. Pop. Pop.

A bullet hit the dash above the radio.

"Keep your head down!"

A male jogger darted out of the way, knocking over trash cans, and yelled something at them as they passed.

The pursuing truck had slowed to get around the car, but then resumed its speed.

They had to get out of the residential neighborhood. The road was divided with a grassy median, and Luke floored the gas pedal to get around a delivery truck. Small trees decorated the median, and he plowed over them and his vehicle kicked up mud behind them.

"You've got to get out of here, Luke. Too many houses. You're going to hurt somebody."

A rock side road appeared ahead between two houses on corner lots. He took the turn at a fast speed, his tires hitting the edge of the ditch with a jolt, but he kept the pedal pressed down and managed to stay on the road.

Kylie sat up taller and looked behind her.

"I said to keep your head down." He maneuvered his truck back into the middle of the road and handed his cell phone to her. "Call O'Neill. He's on speed dial. Put it on speaker."

She did as he asked.

"Ranger O'Neill," Jax said.

"Shots fired at us. Being pursued by a black Chevrolet four-door pickup." He gave their location and the direction they were headed. "Need backup."

"On my way. Keep me informed."

Kylie sunk down but stayed where she could see out. This was his fault. Luke never should have brought the nanny into this mess. She was an innocent victim. He should have sent her out of town after her camper burned, or at least left her at his parents.

White dust kicked up behind them, creating a huge white cloud that limited his view of the pursuing black truck. He knew it still had to be back there. The houses were spaced farther apart and set back from the road as he sped out of town.

Kylie said, "Watch out."

A yellow coupe pulled out in front of him. His truck bore down on the tiny vehicle. If he didn't want to get rammed from behind, he didn't have a choice but to go around. The narrow road didn't leave room. Slowing down a bit, he careened into the ditch on the right. Mud and grass flew into the air. He held on tight to the jerking steering wheel. A teenage girl in the car gawked at him as they passed her.

"Culvert."

With no time to get back on the road, he sped up the far side of the ditch alongside a barbwire fence. T-posts scraped the side of his truck, the screeching sound announcing he'd need a new paint job. The teenage girl was frightened, no doubt, and slowed down to almost a stop, so he steered back onto the rock road.

"You scared that girl half to death," Kylie said. "What am I saying? You scared *me* half to death."

"Sorry. Better than getting shot."

His nanny looked behind them and cringed. "I hope that guy doesn't hit her."

Luke glanced in his mirror, but all he could see was dust. They needed to get to a deserted location.

An intersection appeared in front of them. A county highway.

He looked both ways. Clear to his right, but a pickup pulling a cattle trailer approached from the left. No way to turn right without pulling out in front the vehicle, so he floored it. He'd have a good chance of losing his pursuer if he beat this truck.

"Truck and trailer to the left." Kylie pointed. "Stop."

"Hang on."

"You can't make it."

It was going to be close. He repeated, "Hang on." As Luke drew closer, he realized the truck and cattle trailer were going faster than he originally thought.

The stop sign loomed in front of them. They couldn't make it. He hit his brakes and jerked the wheel left. They skidded, spewing gravel. The driver's-side front tire hit the ditch with a jolt, causing the truck to pitch.

Kylie screamed and dug her fingers into the dash.

Luke's truck slid sideways on the loose rock and continued plunging forward. After he gained control, he hit the gas again and plowed into a hayfield. Square bales lined up in neat rows met him head-on. He hit one after another, straw exploding into the air and onto the windshield. Holes and bumps jarred them, but he aligned his truck between rows and they flew across the pasture, bouncing with every dirt clod they hit.

His nanny's hand went to her chest. "Too close. Way too close, Ranger man."

He cut his eyes her way, a smile tugging at his lips. He'd never been called that before. "Sorry if I make you nervous."

"Seriously? I haven't seen anyone drive that crazy since high school. You need to lose this guy."

"I'm trying to do so without killing anyone."

Kylie looked out the back. "He's still following us."

Two young men wearing cowboy hats stood beside a trailer full of hay bales and watched them tear by.

The field ended at another rock road.

When Luke turned right, two more shots split the air. Both missed. He flinched. If only he could drive and shoot at the same time. Hard to do with the target behind him.

Kylie must have read his thoughts. "Do you have a gun?"

"You know I do."

"Can I use it? Just to back them off."

He didn't want his nanny to have to shoot, but better than killing some innocent bystander by wrecking their vehicle, and there wasn't exactly time for them to switch drivers. "Have you ever fired a weapon?"

"I have. Let me have it."

He retrieved his .357 SIG from the holster and handed it to her. "Don't hit anyone. Aim for the grille of the truck. I don't want you to hit wide in either direction."

She sent him a glare as she unbuckled and got on her knees. Taking aim, her body swayed with the truck's movements.

"Be careful."

She fired two quick shots. The black truck weaved, almost losing control. She got off another shot. The truck swerved again and this time the front end came down as the driver hit the brakes.

"Good going. That should back him off."

She plopped back into the seat.

"Here. I'll take that," he said and returned the pistol to his holster, relieved she didn't get all squeamish or excited about using his weapon. "You did well. I'm impressed."

Kylie looked at him but didn't say a word.

A hundred yards down the road, they crossed the highway, then continued on the country road. With a check in his rearview mirror, he spied the black truck still in pursuit, albeit a little farther back.

"I've had it." Luke pushed their speed higher, searching for a place where no houses were in sight. They were still too close to town. For several minutes, they flew down the rock road at an unsafe speed. Something brown stood in the road up ahead.

"Dog!"

Luke jerked left and slammed on the brakes, barely missing the dog, and they bounced across the pipe cattle guard into a pasture entrance. A barn and cattle pens stood before them. When they came to a stop, Luke yanked his gun from the holster and jumped out his door.

The black truck roared down the road in a dust cloud. Luke could see the moment the driver spied him in the pasture. The man hit his brakes and yanked on the wheel, spinning out of control. He clipped the cattle guard and went airborne.

The truck landed on the passenger's-side front tire.

It rolled end over end before slamming into a pecan tree. The vehicle was now upside down, steam spewing into the air.

A yellow Labrador retriever rushed across the road and commenced into a barking fit.

Luke turned to Kylie. "Can you call Jax and give him our location?" At her nod, he moved toward the truck with his gun drawn.

The Lab continued barking outside the driver's door.

"Good boy. Let's see who's in a hurry to die."

Kylie climbed out of the pickup on the driver's side and shuffled to the far side of the barn, out of sight.

Even though Luke hadn't asked her to remain in the truck, she didn't think he was aware of her position. She needed to stay out of the line of fire.

"Texas Ranger." Luke aimed his gun at the driver. "Put your hands on the steering wheel."

Jax O'Neill's truck whipped into the pasture, the lights flashing from the grille. He jumped out with his weapon in hand and jogged to the passenger's side.

The man inside the overturned truck did as he was told.

While Jax covered him, Luke yanked open the door.

"I'm hurt," the male voice called out. "Don't shoot."

"Nobody's going to shoot you if you keep your hands where I can see them." Luke holstered his weapon and moved to help the man.

Kylie inched closer for a better look as sirens sounded in the distance.

The gunman cooperated until Luke grabbed his arm. Then the man went berserk, screaming and flailing his arms. As Luke struggled to keep his hold, Jax pounced on the perpetrator. Luke handcuffed him while the shooter flung curses at them and continued to kick. "You're hurting me. Stop. I'm injured. This is police brutality."

The man's long, scraggly, dirty blond hair swung across his eyes as Luke helped him to his feet. He was of medium build and had a battered face littered with small cuts.

Kylie, her heart beating wildly, squinted at the man's flat nose and wide-set eyes, but she couldn't put a name to the face. He was one of Hal's men, she was sure of it. Finally, a connection.

She yearned to get her iPad out of her Jeep to see

if she could find this man's file. His name was on the tip of her tongue. Jeremy. Jerry. Something like that.

A Rocky Creek cruiser pulled up, followed by an ambulance with flashing lights. Kylie stayed back as Luke talked with the local police and Jax guarded their man while the paramedics checked him out.

When questioned, the gunman's only words were "I want my lawyer."

Almost an hour later, Luke returned to his truck. The ambulance had left over thirty minutes ago, but Kylie knew how long it took to process the suspect and do paperwork.

The way Luke's dark eyes fixed on her was unnerving. "How did you do it?"

"What?" She swallowed.

"Come here." He motioned with his finger for her to follow. She trekked behind him as he strode to the black truck, now attached to a wrecker. "That."

Her gaze followed his pointed finger to the hood ornament. In her peripheral vision, she saw Jax standing off to the side, watching. Evidently, he was interested in her answer, too.

"No bigger than a hand's width." Luke held his palm in the air, supposedly so she wouldn't misunderstand. "I asked you to aim at the grille, and you put three shots within a four-inch diameter."

She shrugged. "I did as you asked. Don't get huffy. I told you I knew how to shoot."

He squinted as he scrutinized her. "Yeah." He turned to go back to his truck. "Let's go."

As Kylie headed in his direction, Jax mumbled, "That's fine shooting."

"Thanks," she whispered and smiled. She hurried

across the barnyard to catch Luke. She wanted to get
back to his folks' house and her laptop. No, wait, it'd
burned. She'd just have to see what files she'd saved on
her phone. Later, she could get her iPad from her Jeep.
She wanted to find out this guy's name.

Luke started the engine. "Did you recognize our
shooter?"

"I don't know his name, but he looked familiar."

"I thought the same thing." He studied her. "How
do you know him?"

"I'm not certain. Maybe I've seen him on television, or he just has one of those faces." She needed to
be careful how she answered and not mention the endless files she'd gone through the last three years. "Did
he have an ID on him?"

"No." Luke put his vehicle in Drive and pulled onto
the rock road. "Rocky Creek PD came back a few minutes ago to say the truck was called in stolen two days
ago from a ranch in the next county. No lead there."

The man at the zoo. The man who blew up her
camper. This guy. Were they all Hal's men? She needed
to dig deeper. Maybe Hal had a new crew of criminals
working for him.

As Luke turned left onto the highway in the direction of town, she asked, "So where to now?"

"I'm dropping you off at my folks' and then I'm
going to pay Alcott a visit."

Her head snapped around to look at him. "You're
going to check him out?"

He nodded.

"What made you change your mind?" Hope filled
her. Hal, ever the do-gooder, had a long list of friends.

Was it too much to think someone might believe he could be guilty?

"It's not like we haven't looked at him before, Kylie."

Luke said it nonchalantly, but he wasn't fooling her. Just like Hal had done to a lot of people, the killer had made an impression on Luke and his family.

He continued, "Megan's husband worked for him. We've overlooked something and I intend to find out what."

"I'd like to go."

"Sorry. No can do. Jax is meeting me. It's simply too dangerous."

She had too much on the line to be left out of the loop. Like her life. Of course, Luke didn't understand. "Drop me off at my camper so I can get my Jeep."

He sighed. "We were just chased and shot at. I don't want you on the road by yourself."

"And that guy's in custody thanks to your fancy driving and my good aim."

Luke shook his head. "Flattery works, but not in this instance."

"There's no need to drive almost an hour to your parents' place. The twins are safe." Even as she said the words, doubt lingered. Luke's dad used to be in law enforcement, but did Zoe and Braden need protection? "No one has seemed interested in the twins since the attack at the zoo. Which means they were probably never the target. I was. Besides, I want to see how much damage my Jeep and camper sustained in the light of day."

If her Jeep wasn't drivable, she'd rent a vehicle. With or without Luke's permission, she wanted to see Hal's reaction to being questioned. She'd stay out of sight even if she had to go incognito.

"Kylie, I wasn't interested in you protecting the twins as much as I want you with my folks for *your* protection."

"Nonsense. I'm capable of taking care of myself."

Luke shook his head. "I want to be able to investigate without worrying about you being in danger. This makes the third attack in two days. I need to find out who's behind this."

She needed to know, too. "Please drop me off at my camper. It's not your job to protect me." Actually, she could use his protection, especially dealing with a ruthless killer like Hal Alcott. In the police academy, they were always taught to depend on their team. There was no shame in relying on others, but until she could come out of hiding, she couldn't explain why. Once she told someone her true identity, there was no taking it back. She needed to be sure Hal was behind these attacks, and that he'd be going to jail, for her to be safe.

They were quiet as they traveled into town. Kylie made her plan to follow the Rangers. She wished she had a listening device so she could eavesdrop on their conversation. But there was no time to secure that kind of gadget.

The more she thought about the twins, the more apprehensive she became. What if Megan's kids had been the target? Kylie would never be able to live with herself if something happened to those two precious kids.

The twins, or Hal?

Please, Lord, guide me. I've waited for this moment for three years, and now that it's here, I don't know what to do.

"I have no right to demand you go to my parents, but there's no doubt you're a target because of your connection to me. I'll drop you off if you insist, but I don't think it's safe."

Since she didn't know who the next pursuer may be, she wasn't crazy about the idea of staying in a hotel. And since she wanted to be close to Hal, she didn't want to stay far out of town. "Drop me off at my Jeep. I'll go through my things, see what I'm missing, and then I'll be at your parents tonight."

He rubbed the back of his head. "Okay. But Kylie, be careful."

They pulled into Wildwood RV Park and her camping spot a few minutes later. The charred remains and yellow police tape strung around the lot gave her goose bumps and reminded her of the Coffey family's murder scene. Her Jeep was off to the side and looked worse in the daylight.

"Let's see if the vehicle can be driven." Luke's eyebrows drew in. They both got out and walked over.

Her Jeep was over ten years old, but seeing its condition was frustrating. Two tires were completely melted and the rims were touching the ground. She walked around to the driver's side and, surprisingly, it had received little damage. When she opened the door, an acid smell assaulted her.

She opened the console, grabbed her Glock, stuffed it in her purse and shut the door. Then she retrieved her iPad out of a small tote from the back of her Jeep. "I need to have this vehicle towed to a repair shop. Probably need to replace all four tires, even though two don't appear to be damaged."

"I agree. You'll need new tires. The investigators should be through, but if this wiring is melted, it may not be worth fixing."

"Can you drop me off at the closest car-rental place?"

"Sure. Come on." Luke sighed. He started to open his mouth to say something, but must've changed his mind.

She waited until they were back on the road again, and then asked, "How much do you think insurance would pay for that old Jeep?"

"You have full coverage?" At her nod, Luke continued, "Probably not enough to replace it. Did you have insurance on the camper?"

"I did. I called in this morning. They should have a claim adjuster out by the end of the day to look at the damage."

"I'll be glad to pay your deductible. It's the least I can do."

She offered him a smile. Why did everything out of his mouth make her feel guilty? Because he didn't know her true identity. That's why. Keeping a secret wore on her patience. Sometimes she feared she'd blurt out the truth to get it over with. Out in the open. Luke's sister had been murdered, and now he feared for her safety and that of the twins. The Ranger didn't need more added to his burden-plate. He'd been nothing but kind to Kylie.

What would Luke say when he realized she'd been a Deputy US Marshal and had knowledge of Hal Alcott's criminal activities?

If she confided in him, would he keep her secret? Or would he be obliged to tell? "You and Jax are really close, aren't you? You tell him everything?"

"Jax is more than a coworker." He nodded. "He's like a brother. So, yes, I'd say we share most things."

She was afraid of that. And if he told Jax, chances were their whole department would soon know. As much as she wanted to let Luke know she may have information about this case, she needed to be certain Hal was behind Megan's murder. Then, she would come clean. Hopefully, today.

A few minutes later, he pulled into the car-rental place. "Come on. I'll go in with you."

As they walked up the sidewalk, Luke said, "Stop."

She looked at him sharply.

Luke took her hand and led her back to his truck, and then drew her close. He rested his hand on her bicep. "This is no good."

Heat from the contact burned her skin, and she automatically took a step back. Suddenly, she felt silly for letting his touch affect her. Surely, it was her nerves speaking.

"I don't want you to rent a car."

"What? Why?"

He sighed and gazed into the distance. "I don't like it."

Luke turned his attention back to her, and his eyes searched hers. "I don't want you being alone. Not until we know what's going on. Jax and the Rangers, as well as Rocky Creek PD, are investigating this case. I'm sure we'll get a break soon. But until then…"

"I'll drive to your parents."

He glanced at his watch. "I'm to meet Jax at one of Hal Alcott's new houses. Why don't you go with me? I won't be able to relax if you're on the road by yourself."

Kylie had planned on following Luke to his meeting with Hal, anyway, and sit in her car, out of sight. "Is it okay if I sit in your truck and not go in?"

"That'll be fine."

Now if she could just make sure she wasn't spotted by Hal.

SIX

"I'm on my way to the house on Broughton Street. Should be there in about ten minutes." Luke talked into the mic on his Bluetooth. "Will you be there on time?"

Jax answered, "I'll be there in five."

"Good. Did you find out anything on our guy who chased us from Megan's house?" Luke felt better knowing Kylie was with him and not on the road by herself. The only downside was he needed to concentrate and throw all his efforts into getting this case solved. She was a distraction, albeit, a pleasant one. Once Megan's killer was behind bars, he could spend more time with the twins. To survive as a family, the three of them desperately needed time together. Whether Kylie would continue to be a part of their lives, he didn't know.

"Haven't heard back yet," Jax said. "His driver's license is a fake, but we're running his picture through the database. We'll get this guy and whoever else has been masterminding this whole deal."

Luke glanced at Kylie in the passenger's seat. She stared out the window, but had to be listening. "I want Megan's killer caught, too." Even though his sister's death had been months ago, saying the words out loud still made Luke's throat tighten. Sometimes when his cell rang, his initial thought was it might be Megan calling. Then cruel reality returned, and he'd realize he was never going to hear her voice again. "I don't know if these attacks and Megan's murder are from the same man, but I want him behind bars."

"We'll get him, Dryden. There's been too many attempts. They're getting sloppy. Evidence will be left behind, and after we apprehend them, we'll have plenty of proof to make the charges stick."

But could he keep the twins and Kylie safe until the criminals were all caught? "I know you're right, O'Neill. I can't believe I'm hearing this. I'm normally trying to be the calm voice of reason to you."

Jax chuckled. "Everyone needs support sometime. I'm here. And to give you an update, I've had Dean Ferguson in the field office checking into Hal Alcott's background, like you requested. Ferguson sent me a file of his preliminary findings."

Luke felt Kylie looking at him at the mention of Hal. "My gut says Alcott's clean, but I never want to leave a rock unturned." He picked up his cell phone and went to take it off speaker.

Kylie touched his arm. Pleading eyes asked him not to silence the call from her.

Luke dropped his hand, leaving the call on speaker. She was in the case too deep to keep her out, and he was just flat-out in too deep.

Jax's voice came across the speaker. "You probably know most of this, but Alcott was being brought up on charges for laundering drug money through several of his businesses, including his real-estate company. Lori Coffey, the wife of one of Alcott's men, had witnessed money exchange hands and overheard Hal order the death of one of his drug runners named Baze.

"Baze's body was found floating in the Brazos River. With Coffey's testimony, not only could they prove Hal paid the drug trafficker, but they could also prove murder for hire. Coffey died in an explosion along with her two kids and a Deputy US Marshal at a safe house before she could testify." Jax sighed. "You know, the Feds and US Marshals should've looked into the incident."

"I know. We'll keep digging." Luke clicked off, then said to Kylie, "Hopefully, we'll learn something today."

She whispered, "Yeah."

Luke turned onto Broughton Street, a poor area of town plagued with drugs and crime. Elderly folks who couldn't afford to move constantly had their homes broken into or vandalized. A line of vehicles parked along the street caught Luke's attention, and he drove that way. A large wooden sign planted in the freshly sodded yard read Homes with a Heart, and underneath, in small letters, A Hal Alcott Company.

Luke pulled in behind Jax's truck and cut the engine. The new home boasted white vinyl siding with barn-red shutters, and a neat matching storage building inside a fenced backyard. New landscaping consisted of oak trees, various flowers and cedar mulch, and was a welcome sight to the run-down neighborhood. Kitty-corner from this house sat another neat home built by Alcott's company.

Bringing down Santa Claus would be easier.

He turned to Kylie. "This shouldn't take long. If you need to turn on—"

"Could you park up the street? Maybe behind that work truck?" She pointed.

Luke paused with his hand on the door. "What?" A white truck with a ladder rack and three toolboxes sat on the far side of the house, shielded by a large pecan tree. "You're right. It'll be cooler in the shade."

He moved his truck as close to the other vehicle as he could get. "This should be better." What had he started to say before she interrupted? "Oh, and I was going to tell you, I'll leave the keys in the ignition in case you need to turn on the air-conditioning."

She smiled. "Thank you. This is much better."

Jax met Luke as he stepped out of his truck and glanced at Kylie. "She not going in?"

Luke shook his head. "Nah."

"Good." They strode toward the house. "Where did you find your nanny?"

"Nanny service." Jax didn't normally ask chitchat type of questions, so Luke asked him flat out, "Why?"

"I get the feeling I've seen her before." He shrugged. "Maybe not."

"She came highly recommended."

Jax nodded, indicating Alcott. "I'll let you do most of the talking."

Alcott, dressed in a Ralph Lauren polo pullover and khakis, and wearing leather gloves, scooped cedar bark with a shovel from a wheelbarrow. He looked up as they approached and leaned against the shovel. "Hello."

Did Hal really need to assist with the yard work? Or was this for show? A kind of community relations. Luke extended his hand. "Mr. Alcott."

The businessman removed his gloves and accepted the gesture. "Been a long time, Dryden. What brings you by? Hopefully, not official business."

The man didn't waste time but shot straight, an attribute Luke could respect. "Actually, this is not a social call."

Luke watched Alcott's dark eyes for a hint of nervousness when he introduced him to Jax. The bright look. The smile. He didn't pick up any bad vibes. Luke was considered one of the best by his coworkers for reading people and was told his carefree disposition made people relax and let down their defenses.

He hoped his manners worked on Hal Alcott.

Hal smiled. "Why don't we go get a cup of coffee or a cinnamon roll over at that new place on Vermont Avenue?"

"This shouldn't take long."

"All right. Well, come on in." The warmth of Alcott's smile seemed genuine.

They followed him through the wooden door. Plastic sheeting covered the laminate floors and the smell of paint lingered.

"Excuse the mess. We're still trying to finish up last-minute details before the unveiling tomorrow. Come on back here." Hal led them down a narrow hallway to a bedroom.

French doors led out to a small deck. Two water barrels stacked on each other formed a waterfall on the deck, which was accented with potted flowers and green plants. Three large windows on the other wall let in light, making the room feel spacious and clean. A small wooden desk sat in the corner, in front of the windows, with an array of large rolled-up papers, pens and business cards all with the Alcott Real Estate logo. Luke hated to admit it, but the serene picture fit the legitimate-businessman image.

"Have a seat." Alcott indicated the small leather chair

across from his desk. He glanced at Jax and shoved an office chair toward him. "Take mine."

Jax held up a hand. "That's all right. Do you mind if I have a look around?"

"Go right ahead. My crew has a long to-do list, so keep that in mind."

"No problem." Jax's gaze cut to Luke before he stepped from the room.

Luke sank into the chair, glad Jax had the opportunity to visit with Hal's workers without their boss hearing. "Do you know Tommy Doane?"

Alcott squinted "The name sounds familiar. Should I?"

"He's my brother-in-law."

He nodded. "Ah. Your sister's husband. I read about her death in the paper. I'm sorry I wasn't able to pay my condolences."

Not that Alcott knew the family well enough to go to his sister's funeral. Luke wasn't even certain Alcott had ever met Megan. Luke looked for changes in the man's demeanor, but if there were any, he kept them hidden. "Thank you."

"I didn't know…what did you say his name was? Tommy?"

"That's right. Tommy worked for Alcott Real Estate. Your company."

Hal shook his head. "I don't recall the man. I have a lot of employees. Many come and go before I can get acquainted with them."

"Tommy disappeared a couple of months before Megan's death."

"Do you suspect her husband may have killed her? If so, I have no idea where he might be."

Alcott's calm voice impressed Luke. If he was nervous or hiding something, he didn't show it. "We're not ruling out anyone at this point. We're not even certain Tommy is still alive." Time to move in. "What about Lori Coffey? Did you know her?"

Alcott didn't flinch, but his gaze hardened. Okay, Luke hit a nerve.

With a sigh, Hal sat back in his chair. "I went over this with the authorities years ago. I was completely exonerated. Is there something in particular you're looking into? I honestly don't know how I can help you."

"How well did you know Mrs. Coffey's husband, Brandon?"

"I didn't."

Luke nodded as he gauged Alcott's demeanor. He had to give him credit—the man appeared cool and his gaze never broke eye contact. "Where were you the morning Lori and her two children were killed?"

"At my ranch, getting ready for my trial." His jaw twitched subtly. "Like I told the authorities, my home-security system shows my activities of that morning. I provided them a copy of the tape. I didn't leave until after nine o'clock, well past the time of the accident that killed that family and that US Marshal. Now if there's nothing more you care to discuss, I have a tight schedule."

The man's friendliness had evaporated. Luke didn't blame him, even if he was innocent. Time to move back to his brother-in-law. "Can I have a copy of the projects Tommy was working on?"

Alcott heaved another sigh. "Listen, Dryden, I know you're trying to solve your sister's murder and, of course, I don't mind if you get a copy of anything you think might help. You know me. I've known your dad for years. I grew up in this community before moving to the suburbs of Dallas and want only good for its residents. I'll tell you what I'm going to do. I'll make some calls. I'll put up ten thousand dollars or whatever you need for information that leads to the arrest of Megan's killer."

It always came back to money. They needed to dig deeper into Alcott's financials. "I appreciate that, Hal." Luke stood and held out his hand.

Alcott shook it. "Good to see you again. I hope you find who did this. I'll instruct Susan, my secretary, to gather Tommy's files and send them over."

"My email address." Luke handed him a business card. As he stood, movement outside the window caught his eye. Someone watched them from between the wooden slats of the fence. A splash of red.

Kylie.

She was supposed to stay in the truck. He directed his attention back to Alcott as to not give her away. "Thank you for your cooperation."

They walked out of the house together and down the sidewalk. He gave a quick glance, but didn't see Kylie lurking about. Where did she go?

Kylie climbed back into Luke's truck, her heart still racing from fear of being spotted. The large tree may have protected her from Hal or one of his men from spying her, but it also blocked her view of everyone's movements. When she'd realized her position wasn't beneficial to surveillance, she had sacrificed the protection of her car to look through the fence.

Total waste of time. She hadn't seen anything.

Even now, the work truck blocked her view from

most of the front yard. She spied Jax leaning against his truck, hands in his pockets, looking bored. Maybe he had learned something beneficial from the construction crew.

What was taking Luke so long? No more had the thought crossed her mind than the Ranger stepped from the sidewalk onto the grass.

Another man walked with Luke. The purposeful stride. Perfect hair. Could-be-a-model clothes.

Hal Alcott.

Kylie sunk down in the seat. Even though she was parked thirty yards away and wore sunglasses, her insides quivered. A cold-blooded killer. She'd stared at Hal's face in pictures on the internet many times and followed his activities, but she hadn't dared place herself in his vicinity since the explosion.

Luke and Hal appeared to be visiting. Hal laughed and slapped Luke on the back like they were old buddies. The scene made her sick. She let out a frustrated breath. She trusted Luke, she really did, but seeing him be friendly with Hal, whom he seemed to admire, worried her. What if Luke fell for Hal's charisma?

She hated to admit Homes with a Heart built by Alcott Real Estate were cute. Two more had already sold on this street. His company was in the process of building another housing development a few blocks from here. Nice, expensive homes. A small lake stocked with fish and an eighteen-hole golf course gave it preference over other developments. To encourage sells in the upper-class development, Hal bought the worst houses in this nearby neighborhood, tore them down and rebuilt cottage-like homes aimed at middle-class families.

To Hal's credit, building economy houses instead of

buying the dilapidated houses and raising the rents to run low-income families out of town made him more popular—almost heroic. Even crumbling houses' values had risen by twenty percent, encouraging owners to sell. A drawing for a total home makeover for anyone in an eight-block radius was the cherry on top. No doubt, his profits would be greater in the upscale development once this neighborhood was cleaned up, even after the give-away. A win-win for Hal and the people of Rocky Creek.

Could Hal be brought down? Was he untouchable? Did anyone want him to pay for his crimes, or were they willing to overlook crooked dealings? Even murder.

David against Goliath. Since she'd gone to work for Luke, Kylie had thought she had an ally for the first time in years, in trying to take down the Coffey family's killer. Luke just didn't know they were in this together.

A young man wearing jeans and a Rocky Creek Bulldogs baseball cap approached Hal and Luke while they talked. Kylie squinted. Something about him seemed familiar. Using her phone, she zoomed in and clicked several photos of the man. Then she took more of Hal, his team of workers and the house, so she could look at them when she got back to Luke's parents' place.

She scrolled through the pictures to make certain they were clear shots because she didn't plan on returning to spy on Hal again. All of the photos turned out fine. She tossed her phone into her purse.

A knock on her window caused her to jump.

Luke stared down at her.

She let down the glass. "What are you doing?"

"Don't you think that's what I should be asking you?" Luke cocked his head.

If Luke had seen her, Hal may have, too. She glanced back to the front yard.

"He's gone."

"What?" Her head snapped back around.

"Hal left a minute ago." Luke leaned back and folded his arms across his chest. "Why were you peeking through the fence?"

"I wanted to see what was going on." Being honest couldn't hurt.

He climbed into the truck and shut the door. He turned his gaze on her, his eyebrows drawing together. "Next time, either come in or stay in the truck. I can't protect you if you go gallivanting around. Jax and I both thought you were in my truck. Now, let's go get something to eat."

As annoying as it was to hear she needed protecting, she understood Luke's position. When she was a Deputy US Marshal, she constantly explained to witnesses the seriousness of following instructions. Being protected wouldn't be so bad as long as she remembered not to get used to it.

Luke and Kylie traveled the short distance to the diner in silence.

He pulled around the back of the local hamburger joint and opened the door for Kylie at the same time Jax climbed out of his vehicle. His coworker shot him a look. "Chivalry's not dead."

Jax quirked an eyebrow that said, *yeah, right.*

Okay, Luke didn't need his coworker thinking that his and Kylie's relationship was anything other than professional. Besides, it was his fault she was in danger. He was doing for her what he'd do for anyone else.

Not that he ever had brought along anyone to his and Jax's meeting before.

They followed Kylie to the corner booth at the back of the diner, where they had a good view of the room. Luke took a seat on the same side as Kylie, with Jax across from them. Again, his buddy gave him a curious glance, but he ignored him.

It'd been two years since Luke had dated anyone, and even though he'd been fond of Abby, it didn't take long for her to become impatient with the odd hours required when working a case. She had claimed to prolong ending their relationship because she didn't know how to break the news to him. Why was it so hard to simply tell the truth? He believed Abby was more in love with the idea of dating a Texas Ranger than she actually liked him. That was one thing he appreciated about Kylie. His nanny was honest and seemed to understand the demand of being in law enforcement.

As soon as the waitress took their orders, Kylie rested her elbows on the table. "So what happened? Did you learn anything?"

"If Alcott is behind these attacks," Luke said, "he is one cool character. He claims he doesn't remember Tommy, or Brandon Coffey."

"You asked him about Brandon?" Kylie leaned forward. "What did he say?"

"He said he has a lot of employees and can't remember them all."

"But what about the Coffey-family murders? You know, the witness who was to testify against him."

He and Jax exchanged glances.

Luke cleared his throat. "You seem to know a lot about Alcott. Have you been doing research on the man?"

Kylie shifted in her seat. "Some. I find it intriguing a popular businessman brought up on money-laundering charges by the Feds went free after his witness was killed. I remember when his story hit the news. I followed it faithfully."

Was it as simple as being fascinated with a local news story? Luke knew some people were devoted to crime shows and believed themselves armchair detectives.

Jax had been listening intently to their exchange. "Did Alcott have anything to say about the death of his witness?"

Luke brought his attention back to his partner. "He has an alibi. He was home getting ready for the trial. Had his movements on his security camera and supplied the police with a copy of the footage. How did your interview go with his construction crew?"

"Everyone sang Alcott's praises," Jax said. "I made a list with their names and will run a background check on each one."

"I was afraid no one would talk." Luke tapped his fingers on the table. "Even if any of Alcott's crew have damaging information, I doubt they'd report it."

The waitress returned with their drink order and placed the glasses on the table. After she left to serve other customers, Luke threw his hands in the air. "I don't understand what these guys want. Why target me? Do they believe I have something of Megan's? Maybe none of this has to do with Tommy and his employer. Or maybe it's someone from a past case."

"Let's go over this again. You weren't around on the first attack, only Kylie and the twins. The attacker, a local thug named Trey Rigsby, was shot at the dollar store by an unknown assailant."

"Correct. I looked at Rigsby's arrest record this morning. I don't recognize the man and it was the sheriff's department who arrested him for drug possession and a couple of misdemeanors. Not the Texas Rangers." Luke turned to Kylie. "Did you know him?"

She shook her head. "Never heard of him before the assault."

"We don't have an ID on the man with the ski mask who shot Rigsby," Jax said, picking up where he left off. "Nor the man driving the red Dodge Charger who burned Kylie's camper. Neither you nor your sister's kids were around."

"Right," Luke said. "And then there's the man who shot at us today in the stolen truck. That's four attackers, unless one of these guys pulled more than one of the hits."

Jax took a long look at Kylie. "You're the common denominator. Did you recognize any of these men?"

"No." She sat straight in the booth, removing her elbows from the table. "The guy who chased us from Megan's house today looked familiar, but I'm not certain where I know him from. I hope his name will come to me."

Jax was barking up the wrong tree. Luke couldn't sit by and watch his buddy interrogate her. "Kylie's only in this mess because she works for me."

His coworker narrowed his eyes. "I'm only pointing out the obvious. Trying to follow the facts, and right now, we're short in that department. What's to gain from burning her camper? Were they trying to kill or scare her? And why your nanny?"

Kylie paled and grew quiet, and Luke doubted if he should've brought her along. Being chased and shot at was enough stress for one day.

The waitress carried three plates of burgers and fries to their booth. "Ketchup is on the table. Do you need anything else?"

Jax smiled. "No, ma'am. Thank you."

After the waitress walked away, Luke lowered his voice. "Maybe Megan's killer believes Kylie and I are a couple and wants to hurt me. Perhaps that's why Megan was killed. Because of me." He didn't look at Kylie to get her reaction. Just saying they could be a couple out loud caused his mouth to go dry.

"We went through all your cases after Megan died. There were no feasible suspects."

"Look again." Luke tapped his foot under the table trying to rein in his frustration. "Someone murdered her for a reason."

"I will. But you need to keep an open mind."

No one had to tell Luke to keep an open mind. He wanted to find Megan's killer more than anyone. And if someone was targeting his nanny, he'd do everything in his power to keep Kylie safe.

SEVEN

When Kylie walked through the front door with Luke, they found his folks' house dark, with only a lamp on in the corner of the living room.

"Looks like everyone's already in bed." Luke switched on the kitchen light.

"No, they're not. I'm up." Dottie padded out of the back bedroom in pajama pants and an oversize shirt that read I'd Rather Be Gardening. She spoke quietly. "There's leftovers in the fridge if you're hungry."

"No, thanks," Luke said, and held up a small bag. "We went by my house and I grabbed some clean clothes. I'm going to take a shower and clean up."

Kylie watched him head down the hallway. The drive home had been quiet, both of them lost in their own thoughts. She turned her attention to his mom. "Thank you for the offer. We stopped by the store and bought me a few things, and I probably need to shower, too. Besides, we had a hamburger and fries. I couldn't eat another bite." Actually, Kylie hadn't eaten much for dinner. The topic of conversation had ruined her appetite.

"There's Texas sheet cake if you change your mind."

"Okay. I'll take a slice." The words were out before

Kylie could stop them. She laughed at Dottie's surprised expression. "I haven't had homemade chocolate cake in a long time."

Dottie grinned and patted her shoulder as she went to get the dessert. "You want a glass of milk to go with that?"

"Sounds wonderful." Kylie hadn't eaten Texas sheet cake in years. Her dad loved big meals with desserts, and that pleased her mom just fine. Her mom claimed what she wanted most out of life was lots of kids and family gatherings around the table. Simple things.

Dottie placed the plate and glass on the table, and then sat across from her. "Oh, dear, what's wrong?"

Kylie took a big mouthful of cake to hide her discomfort and tried to blink back the tears, but a few drops seeped out against her will. Ever since she'd learned of her mom's cancer, Kylie had been struck with the realization she might not ever see her mom alive again. Never taste her mom's cooking again. Never get to take her on a vacation like she had promised her. No matter how determined Kylie was to come out of hiding, it might not be soon enough. She swallowed. "Nothing. I guess it's been a long day."

"It's been tough on everybody, especially you." Dottie brushed a hair away from Kylie's face. "A few tears never hurt anyone. My son will figure this mess out. Luke's good at his job. Real good."

"I can see that he loves his work." Thick chocolate frosting clung to her fork, and she paused before taking another bite. "I'm ready to get this behind me."

"Of course. If you think you'd be safer somewhere farther away from the danger, I'm sure Luke wouldn't mind if you stayed with family. We can help with the twins." The older woman frowned. "You do have family, don't you?"

Well, now she felt silly. Here she was sitting at the table of a woman who'd lost a daughter to murder only a few months ago and getting all emotional. She should be the one consoling her. *Get a grip*, she chided herself. Kylie smiled and nodded. "My dad passed away a few years ago, but I still have my mom, two brothers and three sisters."

"I thought you didn't have much family." Luke strode into the kitchen barefoot wearing a T-shirt and a fresh pair of jeans. His hair was wet and messy, like he'd combed it with his fingers.

Kylie wiped her face. What had she told Luke about her family? "I think I told you I hadn't seen my family in a while. But there's a lot of us."

"Hmm. You don't talk about them much." He grabbed a plate from the cabinet and cut himself a piece of cake. "Looks great, Mom."

"Thank you." Dottie watched them as they ate, her gaze bouncing between the two of them. When Kylie shoved away her plate, his mom asked, "Would you like more?"

She leaned back. "Yes, but I'm going to say no. That was absolutely delicious."

The older woman smoothed out a paper napkin on the table. "Did you learn anything helpful?"

"You know how it is, Mom. We're gathering information and won't know what we have until we go through it."

"Hold on." Kylie jumped up from the table, retrieved her cell and held it out for Dottie to see. "Do you recognize any of these men?"

Luke cut his eyes toward Kylie before looking over his mom's shoulder.

"I don't believe so." Dottie pursed her lips together. "Nope, I'm certain I don't know any of these men."

"Do you mind?" Luke took the phone and scanned through the pictures, pausing on the young man in the Rocky Creek Bulldogs cap. He ran his fingers across his jaw. "This one looks familiar."

The same guy Kylie thought she recognized. "I thought so, too."

"I'll have Jax research him first." Luke tapped the screen. He got up from the table and placed his plate in the sink. "I'm going to bed. Kylie, do you have everything you need?"

"I'm good." If that was true, why did she have the desire to ask him to stay and discuss the case? Surely because her thoughts were consumed with learning more about the suspects, and not that she'd miss his company. "See you in the morning."

After Kylie told Dottie good-night, she took a quick shower and dressed in the new T-shirt and shorts she'd bought at the store. Since all of her clothes burned in her camper, it'd take a while to replace the variety of outfits she'd grown accustomed to owning. Just three years ago, she'd had to do the same thing when she'd left her world behind. She climbed onto the bed with her iPad and opened her files. She scrolled through document after document but didn't find the young man. Names that began with letter *J* kept going through her mind, but nothing positive. She ran a search for words beginning with the letter, but her vision blurred. With a yawn, she turned off her iPad and settled in.

Like numerous other times these past few weeks, she clasped her hands together and said her prayers.

That night, Kylie didn't sleep well. She got up a handful of times and peered out the window. The sky was clear, the stars bright. Nothing moved, except for cattle grazing in the pasture. If a car came down the road, it would be visible even with the headlights off in the bright moonlight. Maybe it was because the explosion at the safe house where Lori Coffey and her children were had occurred in the dark, but Kylie couldn't help but worry about the safety of the Dryden family. It wasn't fair to put them in danger.

She needed to be near the twins to make certain they weren't harmed. The more she learned about the case, the more she thought Luke needed to know the whole truth. She'd just have to trust him not to give away her cover if it was learned Hal wasn't connected to these attacks.

Evidently, Kylie wasn't the only one who couldn't sleep. Several times she heard footsteps in the living room, and once the back door opened and shut.

By morning, she couldn't wait to see if Jax had learned anything on the young man in the Bulldogs cap, even though she realized it was a bit too soon.

She dressed in a new pair of jeans that fit, which was better than having to deal with the hem dragging on the ground all day. Megan must've been taller than her five-feet-one-inch height. She walked out of her room and found Dottie in the kitchen.

"Good morning."

The older woman asked, "How do you take your coffee?"

"Black." She didn't see anyone else, but there were two cups in the sink. "Luke still around?"

His mother shook her head. "He received a call and left over thirty minutes ago."

Grr. Kylie purposely had stayed in bed longer so she wouldn't wake anyone. If she'd just known… "Do you know where he went?"

"He said he'd be back soon." She smiled.

Kylie couldn't stay here all day. She'd go crazy with worry. She drank her coffee much too fast and accepted a piece of toast his mother offered. As soon as she was back in her room, she called Luke.

"Dryden."

"Luke. Where are you?"

"I'm sorry, but I wanted to check something out."

"What? Did you learn something? Your mom said you left thirty minutes ago."

He sighed and mumbled something about family. "Nothing so far. Stay put, and I'll let you know."

She clicked off. If Hal Alcott was behind these attacks, Luke had no idea what he was in for. She needed her Jeep right now.

Kylie marched into the living room, frustrated at the prospect of being stuck at the house.

"Here are his keys." Luke's mom dangled them in front of her.

"What?"

"Luke took the ATV. He left his truck here. Sam's in the shop and will be around all day. We have a good security system, and both of us know how to shoot a gun."

Kylie smiled. She grabbed the keys and headed toward the door.

"Honey," his mom said, following her and talking in hushed tones. "I don't know if you're familiar with the place, but the rock quarry is across from our north pasture, about three miles that way." She pointed.

Luke was at Munson Rock Quarry. Megan's body had been discovered there. Kylie had read about the man-made bottomless pit with perilous cliffs and a deceptively deep, clear lake at the base. She hadn't realized it was this close to the Dryden home, but she intended to find out what brought Luke to the murder scene.

Luke drove the ATV through the pasture as fast as he dared. The land was littered with ravines and terraces, sometimes indistinguishable until you drove up on them. Irritation flowed through him at hearing his parents talk the other night about how the twins resembled the family. What made it worse, is he agreed. Braden did favor Sam. Now that Tommy was potentially out of Braden's life, and Megan was dead, the toddler needed that connection only Luke's parents could supply.

He gripped the handlebars tighter. He'd been an outsider ever since he learned Sam wasn't really his dad.

Luke had been working a cold case where the family believed their missing daughter was alive. After the initial investigation, he'd found evidence that suggested their twenty-one-year-old daughter was living on a beach in Galveston with her new boyfriend. But by the time they located the woman, she was dead. Murdered only three days before.

The case had been a Pandora's box to his family's troubles. Luke had wanted to get away to Mexico for a much-needed vacation, so he'd applied for his passport.

When he'd gone through an old file cabinet in his dad's office and found an old birth certificate, he saw "Unknown" was listed under his father's name.

He thought it was a mistake and questioned his mom. Reluctantly, she had admitted Sam Dryden wasn't his father, but rather a boy she'd known in high school. Sam had legally adopted him when Luke was four and a new birth certificate had been issued. In a second, everything he knew—or thought he knew—unraveled.

In school, he had plenty of friends whose parents were divorced, a couple of kids that didn't know who their fathers were. One of his friends was adopted. But why did his parents deceive him? Why didn't they simply tell him the truth from the beginning? Was his biological father so bad?

His mom used to make comments how much Luke looked like his father—Sam. Both were tall and handsome. Ridiculous. Did his mom believe he resembled Sam, or was it an attempt to keep Luke from being suspicious of the truth? Tightness in his chest made his heart ache. The wind beat against his face, making him feel that if he drove fast enough, he could outrun his past.

He'd always been close to his family and wanted to be like his dad. Weeks after he'd learned about his parentage, Megan pulled away from the family, including him. Then Tommy left her. Then Megan was killed.

He released a deep breath as he maneuvered around mesquite brush. There was no turning back the clock. No chance for his parents to be honest with him and no chance for him to save Megan. All he could do was find Megan's killer and protect her kids.

Munson Rock Quarry was an old abandoned rock

pit on private land where daring teenagers used to go. Before Megan's death, he'd only been to the site once, back when he was fourteen. Someone had pulled the gate off its hinges and driven a pickup load of kids in. Never a great swimmer, he'd almost drowned that day.

How did Megan wind up out here?

Law enforcement first thought she had drowned, but the autopsy ruled that out. Blunt force to the head. Investigators believed she might've hit her head on the cliffs on the way down.

He didn't buy that theory.

Megan had two little kids at home. She'd never go cliff diving. Mom and Dad said she hadn't come by the house. Her car had been parked at the gate. At least one other set of footprints had been found at the scene. Considering the dry weather conditions and the amount of rock shelf, it couldn't be determined if those prints had been left the same night of Megan's death.

He drove to the back corner of the field and entered through an old barbwire gate—the only access to the quarry from his parents adjoining pasture. He eased off the accelerator and checked the ground for tracks. The grass was flattened making it difficult to tell, but one place looked like tire tracks. Or had the last rain trampled down the Bermuda grass?

Even with sunglasses, the morning sun blinded him. Instinctively, he checked to make certain his gun was in his belt holster. Satisfied, he pulled down the bib on his hat and skirted the small brush. The owner of the quarry didn't live in the area and had posted No Trespassing signs on the fence. Not that anyone paid attention to his warnings.

On the west side of the quarry, he stopped the ATV. He wanted to walk the area to get a feel for the land.

Hiking up a natural step of rock, he sucked in a breath. The quarry was even bigger and deeper than he remembered. Spread over eight acres, the cliffs plunged to the water sixty feet below, and the water was up to twenty feet deep in some areas. Except for the arm of an old rusted rock crusher abandoned decades ago, the green crystal water could've been mistaken for a tropical setting. Contrary to some quarries, which housed steplike entrances, three sides of the Munson Rock Quarry walls had been cut in sharp fashion, creating an almost flawless vertical rock enclosure that was difficult to climb. Dangerous place for adventure-seeking teens.

Megan was no adolescent.

A hawk flew across the water and landed on the far side. It would've been a beautiful place if not for the haunting images of his sister's body floating in the water below.

The afternoon Megan's body was found, the area had been taped off and the deputy sheriff hadn't been crazy about having Luke there. Now, he continued to scout around, searching for anything the investigators might've missed. The path to the main gate was covered in tall, unbeaten grass, meaning no one had driven back here. He walked to the edge where Megan was thought to have fallen or jumped from, depending on how a person looked at it.

"What happened to you, Meg?" he said out loud.

His deep sigh filled the silence. If only his sister would've come to him. Tommy had left her a couple of months before her death. Luke tried to ask his sister about it, but she replied in short, clipped answers, always concluding the conversation with "we're fine."

The breeze blew, but in that moment, a strange sound arose—out of place for the normal outside noises of insects, birds and far-off clamors.

He glanced over his right shoulder. Except for a bee hovering above wildflowers, no movement.

Something pounded through the grass on his left. He jerked around as his hand went for his holster's safety strap.

A force slammed into his side, knocking his hand from the butt of his gun. Luke fought for balance, but one more powerful shove to the back sent him stumbling toward the overhang.

Rocks slid from under his boots, and then he caught a glimpse of a stranger's face as he went over the edge. Luke's hands clawed at stone, which tore into his skin. He couldn't find a grip.

He continued down the sheer embankment, groping for a lifeline as he propelled toward the jagged rocks below.

EIGHT

Kylie didn't understand the chip on Luke's shoulder about his parents. Which reminded her, she needed to check her sister's Facebook page again and see if there were any more updates.

The big white truck was Ranger-issued, she guessed. Concerned how he would react when he learned she was using his truck, she tried to call Luke. No answer. She would be extra careful. Being a US Marshal, she had learned how the department took it when you cost them money. Not to mention it'd be a criminal offense. Even though she used to be a Deputy US Marshal, she didn't think that'd save her if she got caught.

His mom had said he was at the back of their pasture. Not knowing the terrain, or exactly how to get to the quarry, she decided to take the rock road behind their place. The morning sun reflected off the hood of truck and she had to put down the visor. She let down the window and took a left out of the drive. There were no other houses in view. Barbwire fences lined the huge pasture. After about a mile, the road come to a *T*, and she took another left.

More fences and a cattle lot, but still no sign of Luke.

A couple of deep ravines spidered across the land, making her glad she hadn't driven through the field. Finally, the road came to a dead end, with a double gate bound with a heavy chain and lock. No Trespassing was clearly posted on the gate. Nothing indicated a rock quarry, though.

Had she missed him? She called his number again. No answer. Possible he couldn't hear the ringing if he was riding the ATV. She put the truck in Park, killed the engine and got out in the tall grass.

She listened. Somewhere in the distance a cow bawled and an engine hummed. How far did highway traffic sounds carry? Shielding her eyes, she looked around. Nothing but grass and trees in all directions. Considering she was in his truck, she didn't want to drive all over the place. If only she could see better... She leaned across the driver's seat and rifled through the console, then found a pair of binoculars in the side pocket of the door. She stood just outside the vehicle.

Using the powerful-looking glass, she again surveyed the area. Nothing but grass and trees. Finally, she turned to the pasture in front of her, with the locked gate. To the north, the ground broke away. More ravines? She squinted, zooming in. Something reflected. Could be farm equipment, or Luke's ATV. She walked over and examined the lock on the gate, but it was secure. She could blast the latch with her Glock...

Kylie looked around. Still nothing.

Was the cloud of dust in the distance Luke? She peered through the binoculars. Between bushes and trees, she only got a glimpse of a moving vehicle too big for an ATV. Maybe Luke had returned to the house.

She climbed into the seat, leaving her door open. As

she went to turn the key, she heard something. Almost as if someone was yelling. She stepped out of the truck. A gust of wind caused the grass to swish. Finally, the wind died down.

There it was again. A man's voice hollering.

Grabbing her Glock, she climbed the fence and jogged toward the north, a faint trail in front of her. She kept a careful lookout at her surroundings. The voice could belong to Luke or someone else. She didn't need to run up on one of the attackers. The rocky trail and the steep embankment of a large pond or lake loomed in front of her. As she topped the crest, a deep hole played out before her. Water filled the bottom. Munson Rock Quarry.

"Luke?"

Grumblings she couldn't understand.

"Where are you?"

"Here." His strained voice was near.

She ran along the edge and glanced over the top. Halfway down a sixty-foot drop, Luke desperately clung to the side of a cliff. "I'm here."

He looked up, his gaze connecting with hers. He groaned, "Is there anyone still up there?"

What? She looked around. "No. No one."

"Good," he shouted. "Go back to the house. Have my dad bring a rope."

She slid her gun back into the holster. "Do you have one in the truck?"

"No."

From this angle, it appeared Luke's boot had caught in a crevice, jacking his foot up waist-high. His face burned red, and it was obvious he wouldn't be able to hold on much longer.

"There's no time to go back to your parents'." She retrieved her phone from her pocket and slid her finger across the screen. "No bars."

"I know. I already tried to call. No signal."

Kylie would try, anyway. "What's your dad's number?"

Luke rattled off the numbers and she punched them in. Still didn't work. Before Luke could argue, she threw her legs over the edge and rolled to her belly, her foot searching for a hold. Scaling the walls at the gym and the occasional hiking trip had taught her climbing skills, but she had always been attached to a safety rope. She couldn't afford mistakes at this height—both she and Luke could be severely injured.

"What are you doing? Go back up."

"I can help you. I'm a good climber." Her foot found a small crack in the wall. She tested it and found her hold secure, then took a step down. Running shoes weren't made for climbing. She could see from her vantage point that Luke's arms were trembling. He couldn't hold on much longer, but she doubted he had the humility to beg her to hurry.

She descended the rock face one step at a time. Her palms sweated, and she held on with one hand while she wiped the other, then repeated. Her breathing came in bursts, and her nerves were frayed.

"Be careful, Kylie."

He didn't have to remind her. A fall to the rocks below would be instant death. *Or maybe mangle my body so I wished I was dead.* She cleared her head and found another sturdy hold. Only a few more feet. She took another step, and as she released with her right hand, the rock her left was holding broke away.

"Kylie!"

Her body swayed back, her hands clawing for a hold, something—anything. Her shoe slipped, causing her to slide down several feet before her fingers grasped a sharp edge that bit into her flesh. A strong hand grabbed her calf, lifted her and steadied her long enough for her to gain control. She clung to the side, her heart drumming out of control. "Thank you."

Pain and exhaustion etched into his expression. "You got a grip?"

"Yes."

"Sure?"

"I got it." Fear made her speak louder than she intended. She took one more step and was even with him. "Let me catch my breath."

"This was a mistake. You shouldn't have climbed down here. Kylie—"

"Shh. Luke, I know what I'm doing." In field training, she had scored highest of all female participants in the obstacle course and third overall. She was probably the best climber except for Tim Veazey, a super all-around athlete. "Do you have the strength to climb back up or do we need to go down, rest and then find an easier way out?"

"I'm not a good swimmer." He talked between gritted teeth.

What? She glanced down at the water. They could descend the cliff and bypass the water altogether, but the wall was steeper than she'd first thought. They might wind up in the water. "Okay. Up it is."

Luke's torn pants were caked with mud. His boot was turned sideways in the crevice, his weight pulling him deeper into it. He was a big man. This wasn't going to be easy.

She spotted a triangular nook below him and stepped down to it. She put her weight on the stone and tested it by slightly bouncing. Should be sturdy enough to hold them both. She found a good grip for her right hand, but a rock barely protruding for her left. Her fingers squeezed tight.

"Okay, I want you to step on my knee and use it to step up."

"I don't want to hurt you."

"I can take it. Go," she practically shouted at him. No malice intended, as fear drove her adrenaline.

His left boot stepped lightly on her.

"Luke, please don't worry about me. Use my leg to push off so you can get your other foot out. I got this. Hurry up."

He didn't respond, but planted his foot, the heel digging into her thigh.

She bit back a yelp and swallowed, gritting against the pain with her teeth. As he shoved away, she sucked in a gasp, the pain sharp, but managed to maintain her death grip. Closing her eyes, she could still feel him, and his boot lifted from her leg.

As the pain subsided, she looked up. Luke struggled to free his boot. No doubt his foot was numb from being trapped. "Hang on tight. Come on."

With a hard pull, his body swayed backward, his foot dropping back to Kylie's leg.

She cried out this time. Couldn't help it.

Instantly, he shoved off again and found a higher foothold. He yanked his ensnared boot several times, and each time Kylie feared he would pull too hard and lose his balance again. A second later, he jerked, and this time his foot came free.

She wanted to yell some kind of encouragement, but she was drained of energy and didn't figure he needed to be distracted. Luke didn't seem like a man that needed coddling. For each step he took, she took one.

Even though she was in excellent physical shape, her muscles were tiring fast. At the gym and the times she went rock climbing, she'd purposely chosen difficult courses. But this was worse. Her battered nerves didn't help.

A splattering of sand and gravel from above had her looking up.

Her gaze locked onto familiar eyes. The man with the ski mask from the dollar store stood on the overhang, peering down at them.

"Go. Take cover." Luke must've seen him at the same time she did. He took a step up, situating himself above her, and shielded her from potential line of fire.

Her gun was in her ankle holster. She bent down, squeezing the rock with all her might with her left hand while the other hand searched for the gun at her ankle.

A bullet hit the rock to the right of them.

"Move!" Luke returned fire.

She half slid, half fell down the rock face.

More gunfire. Suddenly, the Ranger lost his grip and fell back, shoving away from the edge.

She barely got out of the way. "No!"

Water splashed below.

Trying for her gun one more time, her fingers touched metal. Movement above told her the suspect was still alive. She prayed he didn't shoot her first. If she could just reach…

Her foot slipped.

She screamed. Her hands flailed through the air, grasping and searching for a hold. But then nothing. As she fell, she glimpsed the man staring down at her.

Cold water engulfed her.

Don't panic. Swim. Luke willed himself to keep his head. He had gulped water as he entered the lake, causing him to choke and gasp for air. He kicked his feet but continued to sink. His boots and jeans weighed him down.

A stinging on his jaw caused him to grimace. A bullet must've grazed him. The pain wasn't excruciating, but he'd seen enough injuries as a Texas Ranger to know sometimes the pain came later, shock keeping it at bay. He hoped that wasn't the case.

Images of himself as a kid splashing and struggling to stay afloat played through his mind. He would've drowned that day if his dad hadn't pulled him out. How his dad had known where he had gone, he never knew. Luke wasn't going to panic today.

Please, God, save me. Help me to relax.

There was a big splash, the force tugging him under, and then legs danced in front of him.

Holding his breath, he kicked and used his hands to thrust his body. He soared upward and broke the surface again. He coughed, took a deep breath and coughed again. His heart raced, but he knew in that moment, he wasn't going under again.

"Are you okay?"

He looked into Kylie's wet face, concern in her blue eyes. "Yes."

She didn't look certain, but said, "Come on. This way."

"Wait." He looked up at the cliff's edge, but the shooter was gone. At least for now. "Are you hurt?"

Kylie shook her head. "No. But I think you hit him. The man was holding his hand."

Luke didn't reply. He needed to scour the area as soon as they were out of this pit. They had to get this guy. Concentrating on swimming—if you could call it swimming, since it was more like dog-paddling—he kept moving toward the shore.

Kylie glanced back at him, and then she was at the water's edge. She tried to step out, but her foot slipped and she went back under. A second later she surfaced again. After another failed attempt, she called, "This isn't going to work. Too steep."

Luke swallowed as he concentrated on staying afloat. The little fish who chanted to continue swimming from one of the twins' movies played through his head. Okay, he was losing it.

He watched with dread as his nanny took off swimming toward the other side. She stayed close to the water's edge, but there was no shore. No place to rest. Drawing in a deep breath, he continued to move in the same direction as Kylie.

The distance between them increased. His boots were getting heavier by the second. The sun reflected on the still water. At least he was thankful the water was calm, with barely a ripple.

"Come on," Kylie yelled to him.

He looked up and saw her holding on to the old rock crusher. Surely, he could make it that far. Twenty yards past the decaying machine was the old road that trucks used to escape this death trap, now crumbling from rain and time. There'd be no way to drive a vehicle on the steep trail, but they should be able to climb out.

His legs cramped and his mouth dipped below the surface, causing him to gulp a mouthful. He spit and continued to move. Silently, he prayed to God. *Please help me. I need to get back to the twins.* Suddenly, the image of his parents went through his mind. The arguing. The hard feelings. He needed to make amends with his parents. When had things gone so wrong in his life? *Help me.*

"You're almost here." Kylie clung to the side.

Her voice encouraged him. He was going to make it. Just a few more strokes. He sucked in more water but continued to move. No doubt his lack of form used too much energy. If he ever got out of here alive, he would take swimming lessons.

"Take a rest."

He looked up and Kylie was right in front of him. What a beautiful sight. Her wet hair clung to her, but those blue eyes connected with his, giving him strength. One more kick and his hand touched hers. Relief flowed through him as she pulled him toward safety. Every muscle trembled as he hugged the side of the heavy contraption.

"Boots are not conducive for swimming."

"You think?" He chuckled. He looked into those dancing blue eyes and wondered if she knew how scared he'd been.

She smiled back.

He lifted himself on top of the metal shelf, his boot finding a sturdy landing. A bar stretched across in front of him and he used it to hold on. He'd feel much better when he was out of this pit.

Kylie removed her cell from her back pocket and water poured out. "Guess this is useless."

"Mine is on my ATV. I'll get you a new one as soon as we get out of here."

"You don't have to buy me one, but I appreciate the offer. We should be able to get out over there." She pointed to the old road that he'd spotted earlier. She nodded to the old piece of machinery. "What is this, anyway?"

"A crusher. It breaks up big hunks of rock into small pieces that can be loaded in trucks and hauled out. This machine is ancient."

"You can tell by all the rust. No wonder they didn't drag it out of here. Makes me wonder if it was broken-down before the quarry even closed."

"Could be. Dad said it closed in the seventies. I always remember the quarry being full of water. That's why my parents always warned us kids not to come out here."

"It's almost pretty," she said wistfully. "A house on top of that hill over there would be absolutely gorgeous."

Megan died here. He didn't want to have anything to do with this place. His thoughts must've shown on his face, for Kylie suddenly got a funny expression.

"Sorry. I wasn't thinking."

"I understand." She didn't go on about putting her foot in her mouth. It was one thing he liked about her. Some people actually made a situation worse by not letting it go. They liked to talk and talk, but not Kylie.

She drew a deep breath. "I'm going to sit down a

minute." With both hands, she pulled herself onto the lip surrounding a big metal hopper. "If I can get up here."

Luke reached to help her up, his hand grazing her arm, when she rolled over onto the useless equipment. It was an innocent brush, but the burn of the touch remained noticeably long. Well, now he was really cracking up. Must be the near-death experience that made him react in a weird way. "Thank you for helping me get my foot unstuck on the cliff."

"No problem."

"Where did you learn to climb like that?"

She looked out at the water. "I used to work out at the gym a lot."

"It paid off. For me, at least. First, I get my boot stuck and then I'm a terrible swimmer. You must think I'm a pathetic Ranger."

"No way. Everyone has their days. Even a Texas Ranger."

"Don't say that to my team members." Some people thought law enforcers were some kind of heroes. Maybe that was just in the movies and cop shows. The truth was he did work with a lot of smart officers, but at the end of the day, they were all just people.

She smirked, and suddenly he felt silly for mentioning it.

"You're a good law officer."

"You don't even know me." Luke watched as a drop of water rolled down her face. He was tempted to wipe it away, but didn't want her to think he was crossing a professional line. "You watch a lot of TV dramas?"

Again, she glanced away. "I can just tell."

He'd regained his energy. It was time to go. Wouldn't this look great if Jax O'Neill showed up right now. His coworker would good-naturedly harass him because his nanny had helped rescue him. Luke stepped back into the water. "I'm rested."

"Me, too. But I wasn't swimming in cowboy boots." She plopped down into water and instantly jerked her arm. "Ow. What was that?"

Luke moved her way, pushing around the side of the conveyor. "What?"

Kylie grabbed her arm—blood trickled from the back of it. "Something sharp sticking out."

"Let me see." The cut was shallow, but probably stung a good bit. "Doesn't look deep. I have a first-aid kit in my truck. When we get back, we'll apply antibiotic cream and a bandage to keep it covered."

"I just scraped it. I don't think I'll need a bandage." She sighed and looked back to what she had caught it on. "Well, at least that metal doesn't look rusted."

A small shiny silver box reflected below the water's surface. Luke tugged on the box. It moved but was stuck on something.

"That hasn't been down here long," Kylie said.

She was right. He pulled again, shimmied it loose then finally yanked it free. He kept his balance on the side of the machine as he set the box on the top. The metal container had two clasps, and he flipped them up and tugged the lid open.

Even through the layers of plastic, the color of green hundred-dollar bills showed clearly.

Kylie's sharp intake of breath mirrored his feelings exactly. "That's a lot of money."

"Now we know what that man was doing out here. And he'll be back."

NINE

Kylie moved toward shore with the case of money in her grip. The clunky case made swimming difficult, and she began to bounce forward on her toes until she could wade out of the quarry. Both of them were silent as they navigated through the water, as Luke was undoubtedly considering the same questions she was. Where did the money come from, and what did the hidden cash have to do with Megan?

The old road ahead of them was covered in mud and overgrown with weeds, but once they stepped onto the mossy shore, relief fell over her. "What are we going to do with this?"

Water poured from Luke as he took the box from her. "First, let's get back to my parents' house and get out of these wet clothes. I don't know how much money is in here, but evidently enough to make murder attractive."

"You can say that again." Kylie stepped carefully, testing to see if the rock was slippery.

"I don't know how much money is in here…" He shook his head. "Never mind. Corny joke. Come on. We've got a long walk."

"I don't know if you caught on earlier, but I drove

your truck. I parked it by the gate." At his look, she continued. "You left without talking to me, and I have no vehicle."

"So this is my fault?"

"Pretty much." She hurried to keep up with him, solid ground under their feet.

He looked over his shoulder, their gazes connected and he shook his head.

"Yeah, and it's probably nearly a mile to the truck by the time we walk around the quarry." Her T-shirt was plastered to her, and she pulled the material away from her skin and shook it out. Her hair fell across her face, making her wish for the short pixie style she used to have while with the US Marshals. Not that she cared. She wasn't trying to win a beauty contest, but she didn't like that dirty feeling. Squishy shoes were the worst. Dirt clings to wet shoes. She'd need to change as soon as they got back.

Her eyes locked onto the money case again. "Luke?"

"Yeah." He didn't slow his pace.

"Do you think your sister had anything to do with this money?"

His steps faltered. "What are you asking?"

"You know. Not trying to insinuate anything, but it's apparent something was going on out here the night Megan was killed. Was she into anything illegal?"

This time he stopped in his tracks, pain and anger written across his face. "My sister was a stay-at-home mom and the nicest lady you'd ever meet."

She was treading on dangerous ground, but she had to ask again. "I have to assume her death had to do with the money. If she wasn't into anything illegal, could this be blackmail money? Or maybe she saw something illegal going on and followed someone out here?"

He shoved his hands through his wet hair and remained calm despite the ache he had to be enduring. "I've considered all kinds of scenarios that would've brought Megan out here that night. But I can't imagine she was into anything illegal or knowingly put herself in danger. I've learned from being in law enforcement that nice people can have skeletons in their closets. But it's not possible sweet Megan was into anything criminal."

Good. "If anyone accused my sister Tina of being into anything illegal, I would never buy it. So if not Megan, then Tommy?"

"That's my thought, too. If only he were here so he could be questioned. This case may be more complicated than I originally thought."

Luke wanted to get back to his parents' house, but he needed to know if their shooter had been injured. The guy would be easier to locate if he showed up at a hospital.

Kylie walked up behind him. "What are you looking for?"

"Signs to see if our man took a hit." He continued to explore the area for any evidence of blood.

She began to help him by scouring the trail to the trees. As much as he hated to admit it, his nanny had proven to be a big asset. She'd found the case of money, and he'd probably be dead if she hadn't helped him on the cliffs. "What makes you think the guy took a bullet?"

"I can't be sure because it all happened so fast, but

he appeared to be holding his hand. If he wasn't hurt, he would've stayed around and finished us off."

Luke sobered at the thought. They were easy pickings while hanging on the side of that cliff. "Hey, I want to thank you again."

She waved a hand at him. "It was nothing."

"That's not true. I really appreciate you having my back." Maybe because he was investigating his sister's death, or the rift with his parents had taken its toll, but he needed to acknowledge his gratitude—something he rarely attempted. "It's not often you find someone you trust."

"You're welcome." She moved closer, but her eyes were on the ground. "Here. Blood." She bent over and looked at milkweed covering the ground.

But Luke wasn't looking at the evidence. Her shirt had ridden up her back when she leaned over. Luke blinked. "What happened to you?"

"What?" She stood and yanked her shirt down past her waistband. "Nothing."

Scars. Red and dimpled scars covered her beautiful skin. He hadn't been trying to look, but when she'd bent over, his gaze had automatically gone there. "Kylie." His voice hardened. "What aren't you telling me?"

"Let it go. It didn't happen today." She turned to leave, but he grabbed her arm.

"That looks like a burn. Did an ex-boyfriend or husband do this to you?"

She jerked her arm free. "Of course not."

"Why won't you tell me?" The scars were none of his business, but what could be so bad she didn't want to tell? Obviously, they weren't from surgery or a medical procedure. Jax had questioned him last night about

Kylie and her background, but Luke had defended her, telling his colleague that his nanny was an innocent bystander.

She glanced at the ground as if still searching for clues, but he knew better.

"Kylie." He came and stood in front of her so she couldn't ignore him. "What is it?"

She turned away.

"Hey." With his fingers, he lifted her chin. Blue eyes full of emotion stared back at him. "What aren't you telling me? I can help."

Her skin trembled under his touch, but she didn't pull away. "I can't."

"Can't what? Talk to me?" First Megan and now Kylie. What did he do to make women not be able to confide in him? It'd been two years since he'd dated anyone, but surely, he wasn't that rusty. Why couldn't people trust him with the truth? His hand dropped to his side, but he kept his gaze trained on her, searching for a hint of what she could be hiding from him.

Her shoulders tightened and she pressed her arms close against herself.

He rubbed his hands up and down her chilly arms. "I'm sorry. You're freezing. Let's get you back to the house. I never should've involved you in this case. You would've been safer far away in another town."

She stepped back, rigid and flushed. "Let's go."

He stared at her back as she walked away. What did he say wrong?

At first, he'd thought Kylie was frightened, but he took another glance. The averted eyes, the slight stutter. She was great with the kids, but ever since she had protected the twins at the zoo, he'd wondered about his nanny. She had training. Maybe a self-defense class, but his gut told him it was something else. Not only good with a gun, but also carried one. Law enforcement, maybe. But why keep that a secret?

Before he had time to consider his actions, he asked, "Are you some kind of law officer?"

"What?" Her steps faltered as she turned around. The blush on her cheeks told him he wasn't going to like her answer.

Kylie's mouth went dry. What had prompted that question? She answered carefully. "No, I'm not." *At least, not anymore.*

He cocked his head, and his gaze bore into her. "Be honest with me."

There's that word. *Honest.* She hadn't lied to the Ranger, but she hadn't exactly been forthcoming, either. She wanted to be honest. She'd been upstanding and truthful her whole life, until she went in hiding. The last three years, her whole life had been a lie. Could she trust him?

His eyebrows drew together, his gaze searching hers.

No. Yes… Maybe. She still wasn't certain what Megan's death had to do with Hal Alcott and the Coffey family's murder. She'd gone three years without telling anyone, so she wasn't going to cave now. She needed to be sure. "Don't you need to call the hospitals or something to see if anyone checks in with a gunshot wound?"

He frowned. "I do. But don't think I'll forget about how you didn't answer me."

She didn't suspect he would forget. But at least it'd buy her time.

He hiked over to his ATV, which was hidden behind

some shrubs, and she heard him grumble something to himself. He walked back out of the brush with the phone to his ear. "Can you hear me now?"

Luke continued to talk, so he must be getting reception. She only heard bits and pieces, but enough to know he was telling someone what had happened. As he talked, she continued to search for more clues that might lead to their attacker. In a couple of places, the grass appeared knocked down, like someone had walked or run through it.

Of course, that could be from Luke when he came through here earlier.

A dark splotch showed on a blade of grass. She leaned over and examined it more closely. Blood. She pointed to the grass and mouthed, "Here's more."

Luke nodded and continued his phone conversation. Evidently the person had a lot of questions for him. They didn't need to lose the spot, so she piled four small rocks a couple of feet away.

After he clicked off the phone, his brown eyes continued to search her face. "Call made. Back to my question. Who are you really?"

She was probably giving away that she was hiding something under his scrutiny. Her mouth went dry. "I'm afraid to be honest."

That must've surprised him, for his head snapped up. "Afraid of me? You can trust me."

Trust him. But how did she know? How did she know whether he would tell unless he knew her identity? She'd had it. She must trust someone if she was ever going to catch Hal Alcott or whoever else was behind the attacks.

"Will you promise not to tell anyone?"

His brows furrowed. "How can I say until I know what you're keeping from me? If you've done something illegal, I must tell."

"It's not illegal per se."

He sighed and rubbed his hands through his still-damp hair. "Someone killed my sister, tried to kidnap Braden and Zoe and shot at both of us. I'm tired. If you know something that would help solve this case, *please*—I need to know."

Always a sucker for the word *please* and she could see the toll the case was taking on him. So help her, this better not get her killed. "I used to be a Deputy US Marshal."

He didn't flinch. "Define *used to be*."

She'd opened this can of worms, so there was no backing up now. "I'm presumed dead. By the US Marshals, my family, everyone."

"Why?" He was a man of few words.

"Are you familiar with the deputy who was killed in witness protection during Hal Alcott's trial?"

"You're that deputy."

It wasn't a question, but she answered, anyway. "Yes. Deputy US Marshal Melody Garner. I didn't die."

"Evidently not." He turned and started stalking toward his truck. "Why are you in hiding?"

She hurried to keep up. She hadn't mentioned being in hiding, but guessed that much was obvious. She plowed ahead, not holding anything back. "Luke, I saw Hal Alcott the night of the explosion. I was hurt. Burned." She grabbed his arm to stop him from walking away. "Fighting for my life and lying in a pile of rubble. Hal strode right up to the aftermath, hot pockets of the safe house still burning, looked at Lori Coffey and her two kids and me. No emotion, no remorse. Not trying to save anyone. I watched him leave."

Luke's features hardened. From anger or disbelief, she couldn't tell. "Are you sure it was Hal?"

"Yes. One-hundred-percent positive. It's why I came to work for you. Brandon, Lori's husband, disappeared after he'd confided in her about Hal's illegal activities. Lori was to testify. Since Megan's husband disappeared shortly before her death, I thought there might be a connection."

"And since you were using my family in your own investigation, did you find anything?"

Ouch. "No, I didn't."

He worked his jaw and his face turned a shade darker. "Don't you think you should've told me what you were up to? Maybe the attacks could've been avoided altogether."

Defensiveness crawled all over her. "If Hal learned I was alive, I wouldn't be for long. Nor my family. He'll stop at nothing." The more she talked, the more her heart raced and the louder her voice got. "Even you said you didn't think there was merit in the charges against him. Why? Because he gave money to good causes? Well, I've got news for you—Hal is guilty. I have an uphill battle. Lori knew of his crimes and it got her killed."

"You were a deputy with the US Marshals. They would've put Alcott in jail."

"Really? You'd be willing to bet the life of your family on it? We both know Hal has that charisma that has everyone eating out of the palm of his hand. I had to have proof in hand before I went to the authorities. My family's lives are at stake—" Her voice cracked. She hated herself for not being able to rein in her emotions, and she cleared her throat. "My mom is ill. I can't take the chance of them being in danger. I'd rather my family believe I'm dead."

"That almost happened, Kylie." He held his head in his hands. "If I'd only known who you were… Are. Melody Garner. Unbelievable."

She wasn't sure what he meant. How familiar was Luke with her? By the curling of his lip, she thought better of asking him right now. He needed time to process.

"The US Marshals have a leak."

Her head snapped up. She knew it was possible, but she still didn't want to believe it. The fact that Luke came to that conclusion so fast startled her.

"Don't get mad. You know I'm right." Luke glared. "If Alcott, or anyone else, found where the witnesses were being housed, it had to be an inside job."

"Or we were followed. Or Lori Coffey told someone. There's no way one of my coworkers put me in danger." But deep down, no matter how painful the thought, Kylie knew betrayal was a possibility. If Hal's money and charisma could convince a whole town—who was she kidding, he could convince the whole nation—of his innocence, then why not a member of the US Marshals?

But who? US Deputy Marshal Chase Barclay came to mind. He'd been the rookie in the department and he'd worked with Kylie on the Coffey-family detail before he was pulled from the case to work on something else. He'd been the youngest on the team without deep roots to the department, but as Kylie remembered the deputy, she couldn't believe him guilty, either. He'd been proud to be a US Marshal. She couldn't believe he'd be a part of a plot to kill a mom, two kids and a fellow US Marshal—her.

Luke shook his head.

Tension tighter than a sweater two sizes too small wedged between them as they trekked to the truck. Silence, except for their footsteps in the tall grass, amplified the rift, as his long strides put distance between them. Fine. He'd asked if she was law enforcement. What was she supposed to do? Lie?

She climbed in the passenger's side and buckled up. "What about the ATV? I can drop you off."

He stripped off his Western shirt and tossed it to the back floorboard. The once-white T-shirt clung to his torso, showing a muscular chest and biceps. He threw the truck in Reverse and backed up. In a cool voice, he said, "The keys are gone. Me and my dad will pick it up later."

She blinked. What had she asked? Oh, the ATV. Right. She had to get a grip. They'd been getting along so well that she'd even started to believe... Never mind how she'd begun to think there may've been a spark of something more. As handsome as she found the Ranger, obviously, trust was an issue. "Luke, I'm sorry." Her fingers touched his arm. To her relief, he didn't pull away. "I had no intention of using you or your family. Hal Alcott is behind these attacks. I've got to have solid evidence before I come out of undercover."

He shook his head and pulled his arm away from her touch. "You're not even undercover. More like rogue undercover."

"Okay. You're right." She threw her arms in the air. "Technically, I don't work for the US Marshals anymore."

"Do you have access to their files?" One eyebrow lifted.

"No. But I recovered most of the documents I'd saved on my computer and iPad." She hung on to the dashboard as he made the turn toward his parents' place. "I didn't try to access the US Marshals website for fear it'd leave a trail back to me."

"I'm certain it would. What about my sister? Do you know anything about her case that I don't?"

Did his tone have to be so brusque? She'd known he wouldn't be happy to learn he'd been deceived, but she hadn't expected the darts to her heart. "No, I don't think so. We're on the same side. I'm on your team."

The clenching of his jaw told her what he thought of her.

"What's the plan?" She had to try again. "I don't want to be fighting at your folks'." At his silence, she said, "I heard you on the phone. Was that Jax? Are you planning on telling him?"

Luke's incredulous expression at her question angered her. "Really? I asked you not to tell. You said you wouldn't unless it was something illegal," she said.

"I talked with someone in the office who is going to call the hospitals to see if anyone comes in with a gunshot wound. I need time to think this through." He turned down the road to his parents' house. "Were you ever a nanny?"

"I've been a nanny or babysitter the last couple of years. And I had lots of practice watching my nieces and nephews."

He turned into his parents' drive. "Let me guess. Being a nanny is a great way to get into people's homes."

Before she could answer, Kylie's gaze caught Dottie pacing back and forth in the driveway, and she was rubbing her arms and glancing around nervously. Kylie touched his arm. "Luke."

He brought the truck to a stop and slung open his door. "What's wrong, Mom? Where are the kids?"

"They're gone," she cried.

TEN

It felt like someone had hit Luke in the gut. "What do you mean, 'gone'?"

His mom's red and swollen eyes told him she'd been crying. Her shattered expression just about did him in. Nothing shook his mom. "I tried to call you. Two men took the babies."

"How long ago?"

"Nine or ten minutes, I think."

Too far of a lead to catch them without knowing what direction they were headed. Luke put his hands on her shoulders to steady her. "Have you called 911?"

Her lip quivered, and she nodded. "The police are on their way."

Luke looked around. "Where's Dad?"

"In the bathroom. He was bleeding a little." His mom squeezed Luke's arms like she was hanging on for dear life. "Sam said he wasn't hurt too bad. They tied him with zip ties. You know your father—he fought them with all his might. I heard the commotion and ran to get my gun."

"Come on. Let's get you inside." Kylie's calm voice didn't match her pale complexion.

Luke stepped back, releasing his grip from his mom to make room for Kylie to walk her in.

"Mrs. Dryden, how many abductors were there?" Kylie asked as soon as they were in the house.

"Oh, my." His mom's hand went to her mouth. "I'm not certain. At least two."

His nanny continued to extract information. "What did they look like?"

"Let me think." She wrung her hands. "White, medium-sized. Both were wearing toboggans."

"Toboggans?" Luke asked.

His mom nodded. "With the eyes cut out."

"Ski masks, Mom."

"Yes, that's it." She trembled. "I'm sorry, I'm not thinking clearly."

Kylie kept getting information. "Dottie, what were they driving?"

"Some kind of SUV, I think. It all happened so fast I didn't get a good look."

"That's all right. Can you tell us exactly what happened?" Kylie spoke quietly, but also with authority. Luke didn't mind his nanny taking over because she was able to keep his mom calm while extracting the information quickly. With every pore in his body overflowing with anxiety, Luke realized his mom wouldn't respond as well to him or his impatience.

"I was trying to find Braden's shoes so I could take them outside to play. I put Zoe's on, but Braden had taken his off. I heard Sam's yell, followed by a crash. I looked out the window. A masked man hit Sam over the head with the metal bar used to prop the barn door open. Oh, Luke—" She turned to him. "I'm so sorry. I grabbed both kids and ran for our bedroom to get the gun, but one of the men busted through the door. He grabbed Zoe from me, and I fought him for Braden, but I was afraid he'd get hurt," she cried. "I let Braden go."

Luke drew a deep breath. "It's okay, Mom. That's what you should've done. This is not your fault."

"Yes, it is. I grabbed the gun but was afraid to shoot. What if I hit one of the kids?"

"Mrs. Dryden," Kylie said, "Luke's right. That's the same thing I would've done. You couldn't take the chance of hitting one of the kids."

A slight knock, and then Jax O'Neill strode in. He looked around the room, taking in the scene. "The door was open."

Sirens wailed in the distance.

"What's going on?" Jax glanced at Luke's wet clothes. "And what happened to you? Take a swim?"

"Pretty much. You're just in time, O'Neill. The twins have been kidnapped." Luke heard something behind him and turned to see his dad standing in the doorway holding a shotgun, blood smeared on his neck. Anguish and anger were written on his face. "What are you doing, Dad?"

"Going to get my grandkids back."

Dottie hurried to his side. "You're bleeding." She lightly touched this neck. "Wait, the blood's coming from your head. That's a big cut."

His dad pulled away. "I'm fine. Head wounds bleed a lot."

"Dad, you need to get that checked out. I'll go get the kids. But you know how these things work. You're better off developing a plan than running off with a gun."

Kylie hurried to the kitchen and came back with a damp rag. Without a word, she dabbed his dad's neck.

He didn't fight her. "While you stand here talking, Braden and Zoe are getting farther away. They've been gone, what? Twenty? Thirty minutes now?"

Luke couldn't do this. Couldn't argue. He never should've gone out this morning and left the kids alone with his parents. The twins needed more protection. But his dad was right—standing here wasn't going to bring back Zoe and Braden.

"Luke and I will find your grandkids," Jax offered.

"Sam, get in my SUV. I'm taking you to the emergency room," his mom pleaded, her face wrinkled up in concern. "Luke and Jax, please bring my grandbabies home."

"Rocky Creek Police Department," Officer White shouted from the open front door as he strode into the room. "Dryden, can you tell me what happened?"

He gave the local officer a quick rundown while Jax listened in. Before he was through filling him in, Kylie let in the paramedics and pointed to his dad. "That man needs to be checked out."

Luke overheard as Jax asked his dad, "Did you see what they're driving?"

"A green minivan. Older model," Sam answered. "Dodge, maybe."

"I saw a green Caravan two nights ago," Kylie said from across the room.

Luke hurried over to his nanny, leaving the officer standing alone. "Where?"

"Two nights ago, when I left your place. The van pulled out behind me. I watched him in my rearview mirror, but when I turned, the van kept going down the highway. I figured it was just some man, maybe with kids, on the road."

"You should've told me."

Jax nudged his shoulder. "Come on, buddy. If the van kept going there was no need to call you."

"I got the license plate." She rhymed off the plate number.

"Okay. Good job, Kylie. Call that in." Luke followed his dad while the paramedics loaded him into the ambulance.

"I don't need to go to the hospital." His dad sat in the open door, but his ghost-white face and his sweat-drenched body said he needed medical attention.

"Dad, please." Luke's world unraveled as he put his hand on his dad's shoulder. For the first time in Luke's life, his dad appeared frail. He couldn't do this. Megan. The twins. "Go get checked out. We'll find Braden and Zoe. Can you tell us anything about the kidnappers? Mom said she saw two men wearing ski masks."

"Two? There were three." He rubbed his head. "One guy stayed in the van."

"Did you recognize any of them?" With his mom being scared out of her wits and his dad getting hit in the head, they weren't thinking clearly.

"No. The little twerps. If they hadn't caught me by surprise." His dad raised his fist.

Luke patted his shoulder again. "It's okay, Dad."

He shook his head. "You know, now that I think about it, one sounded familiar."

"Who did he sound like?"

"I don't know." His dad frowned. "When the man hit me with the metal bar, the other one yelled for him to stop. I can't place him."

"Let me know if you figure out whose voice."

"I will. I forgot to mention, I did manage to break

the zip tie and get my gun out of my ankle holster. I fired a shot as they ran for the vehicle, but I don't think I hit anyone."

The paramedics waited to leave, and Luke made sure his dad was loaded with his mom beside him before he returned inside.

When Luke walked through the door, Jax said, "The police put a BOLO on the minivan and search points at all major intersections. They also called neighboring Parker County Sheriff's Department who agreed to keep a lookout. I talked to Lieutenant Adcock to update him on the situation." Jax acted all businesslike, which had a calming effect on Luke's nerves. "Adcock wants to take you off the case."

"What? No." Luke looked heavenward. "I know the case better than anyone."

"I defended you. He agreed to let you stay on after I convinced him you were acting professionally. But, Dryden, even the best lawmen struggle to not let their emotions take over when it hits this close to home." Jax poked him in the temple. "Keep your head in the game."

Luke couldn't stand still any longer, adrenaline and fear making him feel like a thousand ants were crawling all over him. The clock showed it was ten minutes after one. The kids had been gone over forty minutes. They could be all the way in Dallas by now. Or crossed the Red River into Oklahoma. Or a thousand places in between.

Kylie walked out of his parents' bedroom.

"What were you doing in there?" Luke asked.

"Checking to see if the abductors left anything behind, like a ransom note."

"You didn't touch anything?" The question came

from Officer White. "Forensics need to go over the room."

"No, sir. I know better than to touch a crime scene." Kylie gave a crisp nod. "There wasn't a note, or anything left behind that I could see."

Jax turned his gaze to Luke. "Who do you think took the kids? Who had something to gain?"

"I'm not certain." He glanced at Kylie. Hal Alcott was the first name to enter his mind, probably because he was one of a short list of suspects. "Alcott should be at his opening at Homes with a Heart. Can we send someone to check him out?"

"You think Hal Alcott is a suspect? No way." Officer White's sharp tone echoed in the room. "He's one of the most generous people I know. My daughter and son-in-law just bought one of his homes. They got a good deal." He nodded. "A real good deal."

Luke drew a deep breath. "I'm sure you're right. Would you mind checking him out? Find out if he's been there all morning."

"I'd be glad to. Don't know how Mr. Alcott even got on your radar." The officer narrowed his gaze at Luke.

Alcott, no doubt, would have an airtight alibi. If he was involved, he'd be the man behind the scenes calling the shots. The businessman wasn't stupid, Luke would give him that.

After the officer left the home, Luke watched Kylie walk into the kitchen and pull out a bottle of water from the refrigerator.

Jax turned to Luke, one eyebrow arched. "Head in the game."

Luke didn't have to ask what that meant. But what would Jax say if he knew his nanny was really US Deputy Marshal Melody Garner? Keeping that bit of information from his team is exactly what could get him pulled off this case.

Head in the game. "The money."

"What?" Jax asked.

Driving up to learn his niece and nephew had been kidnapped, he'd totally forgotten about the discovery. He started for his truck. "We found a case of money at the quarry."

Jax and Kylie followed on his heels, not saying a word. Luke retrieved the case, set it on his tailgate and flipped it open.

His partner rifled through the packets of hundred-dollar bills and let out a whistle. "There's got to be several hundred thousand dollars in there. There's your motive for Megan's murder. But what does this have to do with the abduction of Zoe and Braden?"

"Don't know." Luke sighed. "Payoff money. Bribery. Blackmail. Stolen. Your guess is as good as mine."

"Can you get some of the serial numbers from the money to the department to see if they've been flagged?"

Luke took a pack of hundreds from the case. "I'm on it." He turned to Kylie. "Come on."

She grabbed the case and followed him into the house, where he laid out the bills on the kitchen table. Using his cell, he snapped pics of the bills in groups of nine.

Kylie glanced at the clock, then quickly helped him line up the money for each shot. She gathered them back up when he was through with each batch. Her hands shook with each move.

"We're going to get the kids back." Luke hoped his

voice was more confident than he felt. He was anxious to get on the road to find Zoe and Braden, but since they didn't have any leads, except for the green van, and didn't know what direction the kidnappers were headed, they were better off trying to learn who might've abducted them.

"I agree. The more time that goes by, well, you know."

Luke understood. The first twenty-four hours were the most critical. He attached a note to Dean Ferguson explaining the need to check the serial numbers. He'd no more hit Send than Jax plowed through the door.

"We got a lead. The green van belongs to an Abraham Fisher. A thirty-two-year-old male with a rap sheet a mile long for petty crimes, which includes domestic violence and theft dating back the last twelve years."

"Good. At least that vehicle wasn't stolen like the guy's from the zoo."

"Yeah. And on one of Fisher's theft charges, he partnered with a buddy named Michael Malone, alias Barry Goodlow."

"Barry." Kylie snapped her fingers. "That's it."

Both he and Jax looked at Kylie. Luke asked, "You know him?"

She nodded. "Wait." She hurried to Megan's old room and retrieved her iPad. She returned to the kitchen with her tablet open and hit buttons faster than Luke could type. "Barry. That's why I couldn't find him. When he was arrested yesterday after chasing us from Tommy's, I kept thinking his name was Jerry and that threw me off. I have his file. Okay." She continued to scroll. "Here."

Luke stared at the man on Kylie's screen. His stomach clenched. "I remember him now. That's a friend of Tommy's. Big guy. They used to play golf together and occasionally poker. Not certain Megan knew about the poker."

"According to his bank documents, Barry Goodlow's gone through a lot of money in the last twelve months, much more than his thirty-thousand-a-year job." Kylie asked, "What's his address?"

Jax glanced at the notepad in his hand. "Opossum Road. That's on the northeast side of Rocky Creek. According to the map, looks like there's not many houses. Might be a great place to hide with a couple of kids. And the other guy…" He scanned the paper. "Abraham Fisher's last address is on Lover's Leap Lane in Meadow Brook."

"Hold on." Luke opened the map app on his phone. "That's clear on the other side of the county, close to the river. Either address would make a good holding place for the twins."

"I agree," Jax said, his gaze going between the two of them. "What am I missing? Why does your nanny have his file on her iPad?" He pointed at Kylie. "I know you."

Luke glanced at her and a sort of understanding passed between them before he said, "Jax, meet Melody Garner, ex-US Marshal."

The Ranger stared. "The marshal who protected the witnesses in Alcott's trail."

"I wouldn't call allowing the family to be blown up protecting them," Kylie added with a little snark. "But yes, I was in charge of their safety."

Keeping her identity secret paled in comparison to getting the twins back. Luke trusted Jax to be professional, so she'd have to trust him, too.

Jax sent him that look. The one that said he believed Luke was getting in over his head. "I'll check out Goodlow's place if you and Kylie want to go to Fisher's."

"Every suspect needs to checked at this point." Luke returned his cell phone to his belt clip.

"I'll call Lieutenant Adcock to let him know our plans." Jax headed for the front door. "If you find the kids, call for backup before you make a move."

"You, too." Luke nodded his head after Jax. "Let's go see if Fisher's van is at his house."

"Do I have time to put on dry clothes first?" She held out her grungy shirt.

"Hurry."

Luke went into his room and threw on a pair of clean jeans and a shirt. He didn't have another pair of boots, but he did put on a dry pair of socks.

As he walked into the kitchen, he retrieved the money from the table and saw Kylie come out barefoot, carrying a pair of shoes, socks and hairbrush in one hand, and her iPad in the other. "You ready?"

She looked up and laughed. "How did you change so fast? You look like a Texas Ranger again."

"I can't stand wet jeans."

"Me, neither." They hurried out to his truck and climbed in. He set the case in the back seat.

She put on her shoes and socks while he pulled out of the drive. "I pray Zoe and Braden are there. I can't imagine how scared they must be. You think the twins are still in the area?"

"We'll know in the next hour."

At the intersection, he went straight on the highway that skirted the town of Rocky Creek.

Kylie's fingers flew across the iPad's keyboard.

"Hmm." She continued typing for the next couple of minutes. "I can't find anything in my files on Fisher. Do you know him?"

"No. I can't remember his name being on our suspect list, either. But I assure you, if there's anything to find, Ferguson will find it." Luke turned into a convenience store.

"What are you doing?"

"Getting you a phone." He pulled into a parking space. "I don't like not being able to get ahold of you if we get separated."

"I almost forgot about my cell being ruined." Kylie followed him into the store and helped pick out a cheap phone. When they returned to the truck, Kylie said, "I'm sorry about not confiding my true identity to you. I would never compromise the twins' safety."

"I don't want to talk about it." He'd tried to shove her betrayal to the back of his mind as soon as he realized Zoe and Braden had been abducted. But her deception kept returning to his thoughts. How could she have lied to him? What was wrong with people? Could no one in the world be trusted anymore? It shouldn't have made him so angry, but it did. He tried to tamp down the anger, but it wasn't working. He had mistakenly thought she was different. Sweet.

He was wrong.

Given that he was a Texas Ranger, Kylie should've trusted him with the truth, just like his parents should've believed he would think no less of Sam if they'd been honest. Would Kylie have opened up to him if he hadn't come right out and asked if she was in law enforcement? Would his parents have told him Sam wasn't his biological dad if he hadn't found the old birth certificate?

But even as he wanted to punch the wall, Kylie had been a lifesaver with the twins. He hated to admit he enjoyed her company, too. Easy to talk to. Smart. Beyond cute. And with the skills she'd shown at the quarry, she made a good law officer.

Without trust, though, you had nothing.

"You okay?"

The soft sound of Kylie's voice broke through his thoughts like a freight train on a silent night. "Yep. Just worried about the kids."

"Me, too."

His cell phone dinged. He retrieved it from his phone clip, hoping to hear the police had found the minivan. His chest tightened when he read the message.

Want the kids alive? Bring money by 5:30. 564 Paradise Lane. Nanny comes alone. No police.

Luke slammed on the brakes and pulled onto the shoulder of the road.

"What does it say?" Kylie grabbed the phone from Luke before he had time to respond and read the message herself. Her heart raced uncontrollably at the possibility they might get the kids back. A ransom note was better than a cold trail. "We don't have much time. I'm ready. I want Zoe and Braden safe back home now."

The phone dinged again, and she glanced down. A picture of Zoe and Braden sitting on a dirty green couch appeared. Both kids were crying. Kylie was going to be sick. She had to get the twins back. She couldn't lose these kids to a killer. Not again.

"It's four-thirty. Paradise Lane is fifty minutes from

here. That doesn't give us much time." Luke's fist tightened into a ball. "You're not going in alone. That's a secluded area. Going alone is not an option."

She turned on him. "You know I'm capable."

"We don't know how many men are protecting them. This isn't a simple ransom and you know it, Kylie."

She glanced at the time on his phone. "I need to go."

"I already told you, I'm not letting you go by yourself. When we get close, I'll get out and let you drive in, but I will be right behind you." He grabbed the case from the back seat and put it in the floorboard.

Kylie stared at the money, her thoughts running through possible scenarios of what they'd find. As a Deputy US Marshal for six years, her duties had been with the WITSEC program. She'd never been involved in a kidnapping case, since the FBI handled most of those investigations.

Luke whipped out and headed down the paved road. "I know you were in law enforcement, but I want you to do as I say."

"Seriously? You don't trust me?"

"It's not that, Kylie. You're no longer under your supervisor. I have a boss to answer to. I want Megan's kids back safely just as much as you. You don't have to prove yourself."

She started to mouth off but stopped herself. He read her well. "I would never do anything to put these kids in jeopardy to prove my value as an officer."

He glanced her way as he came to an intersection. He pulled onto the highway. "You don't have to redeem yourself to me. You're good. Someone in the US Marshals must have leaked your location."

As much as she hated to admit it, the Ranger's compliment meant more to her than it should've. Losing her witness had done colossal damage to her confidence. The truth was she didn't know how she'd survive if she lost these kids. She couldn't let that happen.

"Can I trust you?"

She turned at his abrupt words. Luke pierced her with dark eyes, searching for some answer from her. Her mouth went dry, and she licked her lips. "You can trust me."

He blinked, still staring at her. After what seemed liked forever, he turned his attention back to the road.

No comment. She guessed that meant he still didn't believe her.

Luke's cell phone rang, and he answered on speaker. "Yeah."

"I gave our supervisor an update." Jax's voice played in the cab. "You're not going to like this, but Goodlow made bail late yesterday. Lieutenant Adcock is sending Randolph over from Paris to assist."

"Great. We don't have time to wait for Randolph's arrival. The plans have changed." Luke gripped the steering wheel tighter as he explained about the text demanding she bring the money to the kidnappers by 5:30.

"That doesn't give us much time, and I'm on the other side of the county. I'll be there as soon as possible. Lieutenant Adcock will understand. I'll inform him of the changes, and he'll want plenty of backup." Jax paused. "If possible, you may need to stall."

Did Jax tell his lieutenant her true identity? Kylie glanced at Luke and he seemed to understand.

"Did you tell him about Kylie?"

"No. We didn't have much time, but I told him about the money you found at the quarry. The lieutenant agrees since Megan was killed at that location the money must be connected. Dean Ferguson is checking on leads on Tommy. Something isn't adding up. I suppose you didn't find traces of your brother-in-law at the quarry."

"If you mean like finding his body, no, we didn't," Luke answered.

Kylie leaned forward. "Thanks for not telling him about me," she said to Jax.

"It will have to come out, Kylie. If Alcott truly is behind all these attacks, we need to dig deeper and will make Lieutenant Adcock abreast of everything. We don't keep secrets."

Like an arrow to the heart, Jax made his point clear. No secrets.

Luke must've noticed the tension and squeezed her hand. The temporary touch did its job of letting her know he had her back.

Lightning flashed in the distance as huge thunderheads rolled up above.

Kylie shook the chill from her body. For the next few minutes, she listened to the two Rangers iron out plans of exchanging the money for the twins with the limited information available. They had no idea what danger they would face, or how many thugs would be present. They also hadn't received any updates on the twins' condition.

A vision of the Coffey family lying in the debris of the safe house impaled itself in Kylie's mind.

One thing she knew—Zoe and Braden would be going home tonight. Even if it killed her.

ELEVEN

Streaks of lightning lit up the sky and dark clouds drowned out the sun as Luke turned off the highway onto a gravel road. A low rumble of thunder vibrated the truck. He checked the time on his radio. Twelve minutes after five. They had eighteen minutes to spare.

"I hate storms." Kylie glanced out her window.

Luke raised an eyebrow.

"Don't look at me like that. I grew up near Wichita Falls. Tornadoes weren't uncommon, and my dad always made sure we went to the storm cellar. Did your family take storms seriously?"

"When I was little, around four or five, they had a cellar. But after my parents moved to the farm, they never put in a storm shelter. Our family plan consisted of hiding in my parents' Jacuzzi tub and putting a mattress over us in case of a tornado. Luckily, we never had to test that theory."

They eased down the small path surrounded by woods. The trees provided a canopy that blocked out the remaining light. Luke kept a close eye on their surroundings to make sure no one was staked out on watch. He didn't know how many people, if any, were watching.

A rooftop came into view and Luke pulled as much to the side as possible. "Okay. Remember, go in slowly to give me time to get in position. I'll have you covered at all times."

Kylie gave him a look. "I'm a US Marshal."

"Ex-US Marshal." The sky lit up again.

Boom!

She jumped, and her hand went to her chest. "That one was close. And yes, I'm an ex-US Marshal." She removed her Glock from her ankle holster and checked the clip. Returning the weapon to its holder, she patted her back pocket. "The text referred to me as the nanny, so there's still a chance they don't know who I am."

"Let's pray you're right." Luke climbed out of the truck and waited for her to run around and slide in. "Be careful, Kylie."

"Would you be questioning my ability if I was a Texas Ranger? Or maybe it's the fact that I'm a woman."

"That's not it. I can tell you react fast and use your head. You're a good law officer, doesn't matter the agency or your gender."

"Then what's the problem?"

He had an intense desire to protect her, that's what. Not only because he had the heart of a protector, but Kylie was also growing on him. No way would he admit that aloud. He took too much time to come up with an answer.

She leaned forward and stared above the trees. "Never mind. I'm used to the doubt. Is that an RV?" She pointed at the structure hidden in the trees.

Luke shook his head. "It's an old trailer house. I remember this place. We had a family get-together here several years ago, but the trailer was in better condition then. Remember," he said to Kylie, "stay outside until I tell you it's safe."

"Okay." She looked up at the sky. "I wonder if it would be safer to wait until the storm is over."

Dark heavy clouds swirled above them. A streak of light flashed and splintered into several directions, followed by a loud crack. "Negative. The storm may distract the kidnappers from our approach."

"The kids are bound to be scared."

Especially Zoe. Even Braden would be petrified with strangers. His heart ached at the thought. Luke handed Kylie the case with the money. She wrapped her arms protectively around it and then fidgeted with her Bluetooth.

"Is it working?" Luke asked.

She nodded. "I can hear you clearly."

The sky opened up and rain splattered the ground and the truck.

Luke laid his hand on her shoulder and talked in her ear over the sound of the pounding rain. "If at any time you think something's not right, retreat to the truck. It's possible the twins aren't even here."

"I know." Water ran down her face.

Luke gave her shoulder one more squeeze, fighting the temptation to tell her to stay in the truck. But he couldn't take the chance of the twins being hurt. "Give me a few seconds head start. And then go."

He took a step to leave, then turned back around. Against his better judgment, he cupped his hands under her chin and lifted gently, his gaze colliding with hers. Confusion swirled in her eyes before he planted a kiss on her forehead. "My problem is I care, Kylie."

Darting toward the trees, he didn't give her time to

respond to his gesture. He kept a visual on the drive and the house. Rain pinged him as he dashed along the row of pecan trees. The smell of wet grass and dirt assaulted him. After thirty yards, he neared the house completely soaked. A green minivan sat in front.

Luke stopped and took in his surroundings to make sure no one was hiding in the nearby trees. The rain came down in sheets, making it difficult to see. Piles of junk and an old car were to the side of the trailer. If it wasn't for the van outside, the house would appear abandoned. "No suspect in view."

"Ten-four."

He skirted the front yard to the side of the van. No noise. No dog. Nothing. The ground became saturated, making tiny rivers flow down the drive.

Except for a small glow in one of the windows, no other lights were on. A wheelbarrow piled with beer cans and a rusty fifty-five-gallon barrel used to burn trash were the only things between him and the dilapidated back porch. Not exactly much protection should someone open fire. Gun ready, he sprinted across the open yard just as loud pings hit the ground.

Hail.

He stopped at the corner of the porch, out of sight from the window. Where were the kidnappers? Surely, they were watching for Kylie to arrive with the money.

Water gushed from the porch's tin roof, and he moved farther under cover.

"Do you see anyone?" Kylie said in his earpiece.

He whispered, "No." Was this a trick? Were they luring Kylie close enough to the house to see if she brought someone with her?

Luke stepped up the rickety steps, hoping the rotten wood didn't collapse.

Through his earpiece he heard static and then Kylie mumbled, "I'm in place under a tree for protection."

Lightning struck again, followed by a clap of thunder.

A child screamed. That was Zoe.

"Wanna go home," Braden yelled.

Every one of Luke's muscles tensed. The urge to barge into the trailer, grab the twins and get them out of this condemned place was overwhelming. But he had to rein in his emotions and be smart.

"Shut up and lay back down," a male's voice boomed. "Get those two brats quiet!"

"Don't shout at the kids," another male answered in a familiar high-pitched tone. "They're scared of the storm, and your screaming doesn't help."

"That babysitter should be here soon with the other half of the money. If she doesn't show…"

"She still has ten minutes and the storm will probably make her late."

Luke glimpsed through the misted windowpanes. Someone was lying on a green couch, but only the jean-clad legs could be seen. The hail had stopped but rain continued to pour, drowning out any noise he might make. Two men were all that could be seen. There could be someone in the back rooms, though.

Zoe and Braden sat on the floor in front of the man on the couch. Their faces were red and tearstained. Luke's fist tightened. What kind of monster kidnapped two precious kids?

Crash.

The earth shook and trembled.

Luke whispered into the mic, "The twins are here." He instinctively glanced over his shoulder. He didn't see Kylie, but she would know to stay under cover. When he turned back around, a man's face was plastered against the window. Luke jerked back.

"Hey!"

Being detected left Luke no choice. He kicked in the hollow door, hitting the man before he had time to react. Luke stuck his gun in the man's gut. "Get your hands up."

Caught by surprise, the hefty guy didn't have a weapon. He shoved past Luke and sprinted out the door.

"Unca Luke!"

He glimpsed the kids as his gaze locked onto Tommy. His brother-in-law, pale and with a bloody towel on his shoulder, was sprawled on the couch. "You're behind all this?" Luke shouted. He pointed. "Stay here."

Luke flew out the door only to come to an abrupt stop.

The man had Kylie in a choke hold, her eyes wide with fear.

"Drop the weapon," the man shouted. "So help me, I will kill her."

The man pressed his wet belly into Kylie's back, his hairy arm choking her as her hands clawed at him. Only now she recognized the kidnapper. He was Michael Malone aka Barry Goodlow. She tried to breathe. Luke stood frozen on the porch step, gun drawn, his gaze deadly serious.

"Drop it now," Goodlow screamed into her ear.

She detected Luke's indecision. He wanted to take the vile man out, but then his eyes connected with hers.

Kylie couldn't allow Luke to throw down his weapon and be at this man's mercy to save her.

She lunged forward, using her hip as leverage. But Goodlow's arm dug into her throat, causing her to gag and cough. He held her up, squeezing the life out of her even though she'd gone limp. "I swear, I'll break your neck. Now stand up."

Gasping for air, she tried to get her feet on the ground, but he continued to hold her up in the air. "I... can't." Her feet kicked and struggled to find footing.

Roughly, Goodlow wrangled her back to the mud. She had to fight him. Her gun was in the mud a couple of feet away from where he'd grabbed her.

Luke dropped his gun.

"Good boy," the man taunted. "Kick it away."

Luke's boot sent the gun flying into the mud. "Let her go."

"I'll take the money first."

"It's in the case," Luke shouted.

"Where is it?" His fingers dug into her wrist as he shoved her head toward the ground.

She struggled to stay on her feet. The money was hidden under a bush not far from where she dropped her gun. *Think.* Once he had the money, there'd be nothing stopping him from killing them all. Ignoring the pain of his grip, she reached for the case, water running down her face.

Please, God, get us out of this.

She grasped the thick plastic handle and in one smooth move swung it with all her might at the man's head. Goodlow must've been ready, for he ducked and shoved down on her shoulder, knocking her to the ground. She shrieked in pain. The case slipped from her fingers and fell into the puddle.

A muddy boot kicked her in the thigh. Pain shot through her, making her want to vomit. There was no backing out now. Her adrenaline was on fire, making her delirious. She couldn't stop. He'd shoot them both. She had nothing to lose. Crawling through the muck, she reached for her Glock, but the man beat her to it.

At the sound of a gun clicking, she knew she was dead.

"Oomph."

Luke tackled the man, and her gun went flying. She didn't see where her Glock landed. The rain stopped and thunder rumbled in the distance. Kylie grabbed the case and clawed her way through the slippery sludge to her feet.

She sprinted for the porch.

Bang!

She dodged to the left, behind a tree, trying to see who'd fired. Luke and Goodlow stared at the back door.

A shirtless man Kylie recognized from pictures as Tommy, the twins' dad, stood in the doorway, a rifle pointed at Barry Goodlow.

"Stop, Barry," Tommy called.

Barry turned and ran into the woods behind them. Tommy fired once. A tree limb several feet to the right of the man fell to the ground.

"Are you all right?" Luke headed her way.

"Fine." She leaned into the tree, water still falling from its leaves. Her heart drummed in her ears.

"Unca Luke? Ky-ee." Kylie turned to see the twins on the porch. Luke and Kylie headed their way.

"Zoe, Braden." Kylie held out her hands. Zoe went

to her, tears streaming down her face. She clutched the little girl to her chest. As she held Zoe tight, relief oozed from her very being. The kids were alive.

Luke swept Braden into his arms and gave him a kiss on top of his head.

Tommy dropped the rifle to his side and sagged against the door frame.

"Everybody inside." Luke stepped out of the way as they went through the door.

He glanced at Kylie. "Where's your gun?"

"I dropped it. I'll go get it."

"No." Luke held up his palm and then put down Braden. "Bring the kids inside and take the money with you."

Kylie went inside, creating a soggy mess on the floor. Not that she cared about tracking up the place. Trash and clothes were piled high in the corners. A strong musty smell meant either the roof leaked or the trailer had been shut up for a long time. The thought of the twins being here made her stomach roil. The urge to disinfect was almost unbearable.

Luke came inside and handed Kylie her gun.

"Thank you. Have you talked with Jax?"

He scrubbed Braden on the head as he passed. "I just tried to call him, but no answer and voice mail didn't pick up. Have you tried on your phone?"

She grimaced and pulled her cell phone from her back pocket. Water ran to the floor as she held it out. "That's two in one day."

"Okay. We'll try again later on my phone. Jax should be on his way."

Tommy leaned against the wall like he was afraid to move.

"Come on. Let's get you off your feet." Luke helped Tommy to the couch, and then he took a step back and folded his arms across his chest. "You've got some explaining to do."

TWELVE

Still in disbelief, Luke stared across the cluttered room as his brother-in-law fumbled to put the towel back on his shoulder.

"I messed up," Tommy grumbled.

"Have you seen a doctor?"

Pain was etched across his pale and sweaty face. For a man who had driven sports cars and lived on a golf course, Tommy painted a different picture sprawled out on the grimy couch in a run-down trailer that smelled of mice feces. Tommy shook his head. "Haven't had time."

"Is the bullet still in your shoulder?" Irritation bit at Luke, but he didn't cherish seeing Tommy in agony even if he had abandoned his sister. The low-down man was the twins' only living parent.

"I think so. Feels like it's on fire." Tommy laid his head against the back of the couch and closed his eyes. "But I think it's getting infected."

Kylie moved across the room with Zoe still on her hip and placed the back of her hand against Tommy's forehead. "He's burning up. He needs medical attention."

"I know," Tommy mumbled. "It's not looking good."

Luke asked, "Why would you hurt your own kids?"

His brother-in-law's face scrunched into a field of wrinkles as he pushed back into the cushion. "You don't understand. I didn't intend to hurt them. I may not be a saint, but I'd never hurt my own kids." He switched positions, evidently trying to ease the pain. "I tried to save them. Honest. Guess I can't even do that right."

Tried to save them? Was the man telling the truth? Luke needed to know exactly what happened. "Talk to me. Why'd you disappear? Why'd you leave Megan?"

"I wanted to protect her." Tommy's usual confident tone was no more than a harrowing whisper now.

"What?" Luke's anger could easily boil over. *Rein it in, Dryden.* "Protect her? You've got to be kidding me."

"Come on, Braden." Kylie held out her hand. "Let's see if there's anything to eat." She took the kids into the connecting kitchen, out of earshot, although still in view.

Tommy's head dropped to his chest as he glanced up. At least he had the sense to look ashamed. "I'm in trouble big-time. I don't know what to do."

"Start from the beginning." The setting sun attempted to break through the clouds, casting long shadows across the room. Luke wanted the twins out of here before dark. At least, Jax should be here soon.

"I stole money. A lot of it."

"How much?" Luke had known even though Tommy was a successful real-estate agent, the new cars and the house had cost too much.

Tommy stared up at the ceiling and his chin quivered. "One and a half million."

"What?" Luke rubbed his forehead. "No wonder someone wants you dead. Who did you steal the money from?"

"Hal Alcott. I thought he was going to be indicted on money-laundering charges and would go to prison. He'd been filtering drug money through his real-estate business for years and that lady was supposed to testify against him. I didn't believe he'd find out who took the money."

He and Kylie exchanged glances. Even though Kylie had warned him about the businessman, Luke still hadn't quite believed Alcott was capable of such crime. "Did Alcott kill Megan?"

"Yes, he had one of his men kill her. Hal didn't learn it was me who took the money until about six months ago. He demanded his money be returned, but I had already spent over six hundred thousand. I never dreamed he'd kill Megan. I promise. I'm so sorry. You've got to believe me. I never meant for everything to get out of control. I was scared, and I've been hiding out at this trailer. I didn't even go to my wife's funeral..." His voice cracked. Tears ran down his face.

"Get a grip, Tommy." Luke glanced over at the twins as they clung to Kylie's wet jeans. Did the man even realize he was scaring his own kids? "Do you have any proof he killed my sister?"

He nodded. "He sent me a video of her tied up and sitting in a car. You can't see Hal, but it's his voice."

Luke's chest constricted and his fists tightened.

Tommy lowered his voice. "Then Hal sent someone to abduct the kids at the zoo. I couldn't let 'em kill Zoe and Braden, too." He had dark circles under his eyes, and his hollow checks deepened as he drew a ragged breath and tried to stand. "I need to get out of here. Hal will send someone to kill me. Protect the kids. With me injured..."

"You need to turn yourself in. It's the only way we can protect you."

"Protect me?" Tommy snorted. "Nothing can save me now. That's why I took the kids. I'm sorry for scaring you and your parents. You're good people, but I didn't trust you to keep them safe. The twins would've gotten used to me again with time. I know you're a Texas Ranger and Sam used to be a state trooper, but the kids would've never been safe with Hal after them. That's why I was taking them to Mexico."

"Mexico?" Luke held back his anger. He needed to know the players. "How are Fisher and Goodlow involved?"

"I didn't have a choice," Tommy said, his voice squeaking, and he kept talking like Luke hadn't asked a question. "They would've killed Zoe and Braden to get to me. You don't know what Hal's capable of. He has a lot of people on his side. Everyone likes him. Businessmen. Politicians. Law enforcement. You wouldn't know who to trust."

"Tommy, stop. You're becoming hysterical. Do Abraham Fisher and Barry Goodlow work for Alcott?"

"No. I paid them to help me get the kids back. I promised them a hundred thousand dollars each when we were safe across the border. I hid part of the money in Zoe and Braden's room and the other half at the quarry. After your dad shot me at the ranch, they double-crossed me. Said *I* was a liability. They wanted the money for themselves and don't care about my kids. They'd shoot me if they thought they could find the money."

His dad did hit someone. Tommy.

"Luke," Kylie called from the kitchen as she looked out the window. "We have company."

He strode over and glanced out the smudged window. A dark car came to a stop in the drive. "Get the kids to the bedroom."

"We'll be sitting ducks. The walls are paper-thin and wouldn't stop a bullet."

Luke couldn't protect them if they weren't beside him. "I need you near me. Use a mattress for protection."

"Barry is back." She looked out the window as she gathered the kids in her arms. "Tommy, who is the other guy?"

His brother-in-law leaned over the arm of the couch and stared out a window at the two men getting out of the sedan, assault rifles in hand. "My partners. Abraham and Barry. They want the money."

Why did anyone in crime ever think another criminal could be trusted? Luke grabbed the case of money. He'd need a bargaining chip if the men decided to rid themselves of all witnesses. "Kylie, get in the bedroom."

"No. I won't chance the kids' safety. I'm taking them out the back door and through the trees. I'll keep them far away from the gunfire."

"Stay hidden. I will come for you." Luke checked his gun and watched out the window until he heard Kylie's footsteps go down the back steps. He didn't want her alone.

"Go," Tommy insisted. He struggled to his feet and snagged the rifle from the corner. "Save my kids. The other half of the money is in a foam ice chest in the shed out back. And Luke, if I don't get out of this alive, take care of my kids. It's what Megan wanted."

Luke didn't have time to argue and went out the back door to find Kylie.

* * *

Kylie dashed for the cover of the woods. Carrying a child on each hip wasn't the easiest way to travel, but it was better than making the children walk in the mud. Zoe clung tight and was silent.

"Unca Luke." Braden held out his hands over her shoulder.

"We'll see him in a bit. Hang on." Kylie's attention focused on getting to safety before they were spotted.

A gunshot went off.

Zoe and Braden both jumped in her arms, but Kylie pulled them even tighter and kept going, heaving for breath.

"Want to go home!" Zoe cried.

"Shh. It'll be okay. Hang on." Was that Luke shooting at the men? Or did they shoot Luke? She didn't take the time to turn around, but raced for cover, careful not to trip on the uneven terrain. Overgrown bushes appeared in front of her and she dodged them. Her muddy running shoe slipped, and she almost went to the ground.

Footsteps sounded behind her. Oh, no. This couldn't be happening. Setting the kids on their feet, she slid her Glock from the holster and turned in one smooth motion. She aimed.

"Kylie. It's me. Don't shoot."

She jumped at the sound of Luke's voice and relief flooded her. "What are you doing?" She tucked away her gun and picked up the kids. "You scared me half to death."

He snagged Braden from her grasp while holding the case. "Getting you out of here."

"We need to take...these guys down." She gasped for air. "We'll...never be free until they're captured."

"Did you call Jax again?"

"No time. He was on his way here over thirty minutes a—"

There were three popping sounds, followed by rapid gunfire.

The second round of shots sounded like they'd come from assault rifles.

Zoe cried and crawled higher on Kylie's shoulder. The toddler shook uncontrollably. "No."

Luke and Kylie exchanged looks. Without saying a word, understanding passed between them. Unless he'd somehow escaped, those last shots were aimed at Tommy.

"Keep moving. We can talk later."

Braden puckered his lip. "Bad man."

"It's okay, little buddy. Uncle Luke's got you. We're going for a walk." A barbwire fence stretched across their path, the trees and brush so thick it'd be impossible to cross.

A noise sounded somewhere behind them. Kylie glanced back over her shoulder. Only green and trees, with a bit of light. She was thankful the rain had stopped, but the slick trail would make it easy to fall. They had to get these kids out of here. This was no place for a shoot-out.

Luke headed to the right along the fence. As he hiked, he tried calling Jax again.

"No answer?"

He shook his head. "No bars."

She let out a frustrated sigh. "Are you familiar with the area?"

"A little. I went camping here when I was thirteen or fourteen. Megan would've been eight or nine. Barbecue type of thing with the family, but we had an RV. A couple of my friends stayed in the trailer, but it was in much better shape then. We played capture the flag in the trees. If I remember correctly, there's a barn out here."

"How did Tommy know about this place?" Kylie stepped across a fallen log and Luke put his hand on the back of her arm to help.

"I don't know, unless Megan told him about it. I don't even know who owns the land."

"Do you think we can go back to your truck now? It's starting to get dark."

"I'd rather not until Jax arrives. Fisher and Goodlow might be gone, or they may be scouring the woods for us." Luke tapped her shoulder. "Right there. Come on."

He led the way to a small unpainted barn covered in ivy and briars. A rusty tractor sat off to the side and the wooden cattle pens had been overrun with trees.

They walked underneath the shed.

Kylie glanced up at the wooden rafters that held up the tin roof. "You sure it's safe?"

"It's probably been standing eighty years. I don't see it falling down today. Watch for snakes."

"Great. Thanks. Just what I needed to worry about." She examined the inside of the barn. Old hay littered the wooden floor and dark shadows made it near impossible to see.

"At least it's dry." Luke's eyebrows lifted. "I've been wet enough for one day."

"You can say that again. I really don't want to find out if anything lives here." She glanced around, glad no other eyes were staring back.

"Down." Braden squirmed.

Luke put him on the ground. "Stay close, little man."

"Okay, Unca Luke."

Kylie's arm was about to fall off. She set Zoe at her feet, but the little girl continued to cling to her leg. Kylie shook her arm trying to get the feeling back.

"I'll be right back." Luke peered outside and then disappeared with the money case.

He didn't have to explain. She knew he was going to check things out. Delayed relief flooded her. She was so glad they'd gotten the kids back. She didn't know how she could ever forgive herself if harm had come to Zoe and Braden.

She bent down on her knees in the hay. She preferred the barn to the smelly trailer house. "You kids were so brave. I'm proud of you."

Zoe wrapped her arms around Kylie's neck. "Ky-ee. Don't go."

"I'm not going to leave you, baby." Tears blurred her vision. So much for not falling in love with these two. How could she not? They were precious as could be. But what about after this was over and she went back to her family and old life? How much upheaval could the twins survive?

"Ah, yaw." Braden did a karate chop through the air.

Kylie rubbed his head and laughed. "Someone's been watching cartoons."

"Where Unca Luke?" Braden asked, looking at the doorway his uncle had exited.

"He'll be back." Kylie stood and stepped over to the opening and glanced out. The sun had almost set and the cool winds from the storm were replaced with sticky humidity. She didn't want to stay out here tonight, but she'd do whatever she had to do to keep these two from danger. What if Luke didn't come back? Should she stay here for the night or try to make it back to Luke's truck?

With the kids' attention on the few old hay bales in the corner, she reached in her holster and checked her gun. Even though she hadn't removed any bullets or shot the gun, she felt better seeing the clip full and ready. She returned it to her ankle holster.

Her stomach growled. She had fed the kids cheese crackers from an unopened package on the counter in the kitchen. The trailer was dirty, but the snacks looked fresh. Now she wished she would've eaten something, too. This could turn out to be a long night.

Footsteps outside had her looking up, her hand on the butt of her gun.

"Looks like we've lost them." Luke stepped inside with the case at his side and came to stand next to her. He whispered where only she could hear. "We're safe for now, but with several hundred thousand dollars in our care, Fisher and Goodlow won't give up. They'll be coming for us."

THIRTEEN

Luke noticed Kylie chewing on her lip, and he instantly regretted his statement. What was he thinking? Even though she used to be in law enforcement, that shouldn't stop him from using tact. "We're going to get out of this..." *Babe.* He almost called her *babe.*

His intentions were the last thing she needed to worry about. Must be the intense emotional stress of the situation causing him to act out of character.

She glanced at the case. "Why did you take that with you? Afraid I might help myself to a little bit?"

He shook his head at her sarcasm and laid the case against the shed wall. "Nope. A little insurance in case Fisher and Goodlow find us. I put the money under the hood of that old tractor."

"They won't be happy if they learn we don't have the money on us. Hope they're patient and not trigger-happy."

"Not much choice. After Tommy stole the money, he put half in the twins' room—I assume in the Lego container you found—and the other half of the cash at the quarry. He told me he stashed what he had left of the money in a foam chest in the shed behind the trailer.

If Fisher and Goodlow find the money, there won't be any reason to keep us alive."

Kylie rolled from her knees to sit in the hay and rested her elbows on her thighs. "Do you think we should've left the case with the money so they could take it and go? Law enforcement could always pick them up later."

"I considered that. But just because they have the money doesn't mean they wouldn't try to kill us before they left. That's a chance I'm not willing to take with Zoe and Braden." Luke needed backup. What was delaying Jax? Luke tried calling him again, but still no reception. A number of things could've delayed him.

As if Kylie read his thoughts, she asked, "If Jax doesn't show, are we going to stay here for the night? Or keep moving?"

"Stay here until I have backup." He returned to the doorway and stared out, searching out the horizon. The sun had set, and the stars shone bright. Quite a contrast to the earlier storm. Besides crickets and frogs, silence filled the night. Luke would like to go back to the trailer to see if Fisher and Goodlow were still there, but he didn't want to leave Kylie and the kids alone.

"Won't Jax be walking into a trap? Do you need to warn him?"

Luke shook his head. "O'Neill will be looking for trouble. He's probably the best Ranger in the department."

"I envy you."

Where did that come from? Luke waited for her to explain.

"Even though I'd been with the Marshals for six years, I hadn't developed deep relationships." She picked up a piece of straw and peeled it into pieces. "At first, I blamed the lack of camaraderie on me being the only female in our division, but maybe it's because they didn't trust me to do my job."

"I find that difficult to believe. You seem competent to me. I'd take you as my partner any day of the week."

"Thanks, Luke. That means a lot coming from you."

He watched as crimson crept up her face. Her skin was soft and touchable. The way she wore her confidence, he'd never guess Kylie needed assurance. How could he be so blind? Of course, she doubted her ability just as he had questioned his competence after he lost his own sister to a killer. "What about the Coffey family? Who was helping you protect them?"

"No one that morning, only me. A new deputy, Chase Barclay, had been with us at first, getting the family settled. Then after a couple of days, he was assigned to another case. I thought he'd be brought back the week of the trial, but he wasn't. I'm sure you know sometimes the departments are stretched thin."

"I'd think that was an important case."

She tilted her head to the side and sneered. "You would think so, wouldn't you? The Coffey family wasn't considered to be in a high level of danger. Hence, Barclay being assigned elsewhere." She waved her hand dismissively. "Hal had been accused of money laundering, not being a drug lord and a known killer. It wasn't until after the explosion and killing of my witness that even I believed the threat great. I didn't know much about the case before the explosion because my job was to protect the witnesses, not investigate Hal."

"I'm sure your boss didn't take that too well after the fact. Probably takes all cases more serious now."

"The assistant director of the US Marshals, Seth Wheeler, was my superior. I researched, and from what I could find, he wasn't reprimanded. But then again, that kind of stuff can be kept secret."

"Hindsight is twenty-twenty."

"True. Do you *finally* believe Hal is the mastermind behind all the attacks? The murders of the Coffeys and Megan? Do you understand why I felt the need to go undercover?"

That uncomfortable feeling of betrayal raised its ugly head like a sucker punch to the jaw. "I understand. Am I happy you didn't confide in me? No, but I understand."

"But if it had turned out Hal had nothing to do with Megan's death, I would've sacrificed my identity for nothing." She looked at him with determination. "Makes me wonder how big his operation is and what other crimes he's committed."

"I'm certain it will take a while to sort out his activities." Luke still had a difficult time wrapping his head around the implications. "The man must have accomplices, too. Thugs from out of town or more businessmen? I'd hate to learn of even more of our local townspeople being involved."

"Good question. He couldn't get by without other people covering for him."

Braden stomped on top of a hay bale and it suddenly gave way. He fell in the soft straw on the barn floor.

Luke sighed. "Time these kids get some sleep while everything is quiet."

"Come here, baby," Kylie said to Zoe. His niece crashed beside Kylie's legs and yawned. Kylie drew her face against her chest. "Time to go to sleep."

Unlike Zoe, Braden climbed on and jumped off the hay bale again.

"Braden reminds me of my younger brother, Ben, when he was that age." Kylie smiled but stared off like she was a mile away. "Ben never sat still and fought naps like it was the worst fate ever. He'd pass out in the middle of the living-room floor, or wherever he happened to be playing, when he finally ran out of fumes."

He hadn't had time to process how much she must've been missing her family. "Earlier when you told me your true identity, you mentioned your mom was ill."

She nodded and glanced away. "Cancer. She has surgery in a couple of weeks. Pretty serious from what I understand."

"I'm sorry."

She shook her head. "My biggest fear is that Mom would die never knowing I was alive."

He detected the raw emotion in her voice. "I didn't even consider what that must be like for you."

"You want to know my biggest regret?" She turned and looked straight at him, her eyes glistening with moisture. "My mom is a simple woman and never has asked for much. When my dad was alive she always wanted them to take a trip to Niagara Falls. Ride the railways. But he died before they ever got that chance. After his death, I promised her that I would take her to New York, just Mom and me. I thought I had plenty of time, so I put it off. Then I faked my own death." Her lip trembled. "I don't even know if she'll make it through the surgery."

"Hey." He'd never been good in these situations and felt like anything he said would be inadequate. "We'll put Hal behind bars and get you back to your family in plenty of time for your mom's surgery. Promise."

She gave him a slight smile.

Speaking of putting their man in jail, Luke needed to check things out again. "Time to settle down." He scooped up Braden and gently shoved his head against his shoulder.

"I've never been able to get Braden to calm down that fast."

"I know kids." He poked himself in the chest with his thumb.

"Yeah. Right."

He laughed. Braden reared his head back and looked at him, smiled and then laid his head down. Luke's heart did a little somersault at the feel of the boy in his arms, as he sat beside Kylie in the hay. Before she came along, he'd been struggling with his niece and nephew. Survival had been the main goal. Get the kids fed, changed and bathed with the least amount of crying. After the second time of loading the twins up late at night to make a diaper run, he'd finally bought five humongous boxes at a warehouse store. Yeah, he knew he needed to do better. He'd always figured he'd have children someday but had shoved the idea way off in the future since he wasn't married.

Zoe's breathing evened out as she fell asleep in his nanny's arms. Peaceful. Now he couldn't imagine his life without the twins. They made him long for something he didn't realize he was missing.

He was a better person with Kylie by his side. They made a good team. And a part of him dreaded when this was over and she went back to her old life.

* * *

Kylie thought the Ranger needed to laugh more often. She'd met a lot of handsome men in her life, but Luke… Well, he made her want to lie on the couch with her head on his shoulder while eating popcorn and watching television. *Stop stargazing at him*, she chided herself.

Luke and Braden really were good together. Braden could do a lot worse than have Luke for a dad. Sadness came on unexpectedly. What had happened to Tommy? Kylie wanted to see what was going on out there. Had the two men left? Were they searching for them this very minute? It was almost in her to suggest Luke go find out while she watched the twins, but the thought of Luke being overtaken and the men finding her alone with the kids was simply too big a chance.

In a few minutes, the twins were asleep, Zoe dozing on Kylie and Braden passed out on Luke. "They're really sweet kids."

The Ranger glanced at Zoe in her arms. "I know. Megan was a good mom. It's been hard on the kids being shuffled around."

"You're doing a good job, Luke. I wish I would've known your sister."

He smiled. "You would've liked each other. She was stubborn, much like you." He held up a hand. "I mean that as a compliment. When you want something, you go for it. I'm glad you didn't keep the twins in the trailer. I'm not sure I could've defended you there."

"I was scared to death. After losing Lori Coffey and her two kids, I should've known better than to leave the kids alone at your parents. I should've stayed at the house with them."

He tilted his head. "I'm pretty sure if you hadn't come looking for me, our attacker would've killed me."

"Maybe." She stared into her lap. "But I shouldn't have taken the chance. Zoe and Braden are depending on me. I won't leave them alone again."

His hand reached and touched her knee, sending electricity throughout her entire being. "The Coffey family wasn't your fault. Someone blew up the safe house. Alcott, or someone else—doesn't matter. You did your best."

"My best wasn't good enough." She looked up into his dark eyes, waves of emotion dancing there. Concern. Care. How long had it been since someone looked at her that way? Maybe never.

"That's the thing about being in law enforcement. You can't save them all. If it didn't hurt, then you wouldn't be good at your job." His fingers found her hand and gave her a squeeze. "I can see you care, Kylie. You're a good officer."

Not anymore, but she didn't say the words out loud. She didn't want to come across as seeking reassurance. The truth was, Luke's words meant the world to her. That family might be alive today if she could have only sensed the danger. Should she have checked out the premises more often? How long did it take for Hal to set up the explosives? He could've been at the house thirty minutes or longer watching for them, and she'd never seen him.

"Thank you." The warmth of his hand felt good. Made her not feel alone. Without her family being near, she'd desperately missed close interaction. They were a touchy-feely group of people, especially her mom.

Luke climbed to his feet and laid Braden in the hay

beside her. "With the kids asleep, I'm going to keep watch outside. If those men are looking for us, the barn would draw their attention. Try to get some sleep."

"Okay." Her hand remained cool except where his warm touch still lingered. Kylie didn't dare consider what was happening between the two of them. Consistent with the last three years, she didn't have time to form relationships. She put Zoe next to Braden, extracted her gun from her holster and looked out the open doorway.

Trees outside the barn blocked out any moonlight, black shadows heavy and all consuming. She didn't see Luke, but she could feel him. Strange. She hadn't known him all that long. Not wanting to drive herself crazy with worry, she went back and sat by the twins. If anything happened, she wanted them as close to her as possible.

With a hand on Zoe's back, she played with the girl's blond curls. Nothing so precious as a sleeping child.

The day must've taken its toll. She leaned back in the hay and closed her eyes. Before she knew it, movement had her trying to figure out where she was. She must've fallen asleep. Zoe stirred in her sleep and suddenly Kylie remembered where she was. The barn.

Scuffling came from outside.

Where was Luke?

That wasn't outside. Something moved in the corner. Her hand was steady in spite of chill bumps popping up on her arms. She slid her Glock out of her holster and gently climbed to her feet, careful not to wake Zoe. Staying low, she waited for her eyes to adjust to the darkness. Nothing but hay bales in the corner. No one in the doorway.

Was Luke still keeping watch? If Luke was keeping an eye on the barn, he should be close by.

More movement.

Her chest constricted. Something was definitely in here.

She eased closer, her gun ready. Two little beady eyes started back at her from behind a bale.

She let out a pent-up breath with a whoosh.

A possum scurried across the floor, stopped and looked at her. Then it took off again and disappeared behind the stacks of hay.

Good grief. A smile spread across her lips and she dropped the gun to her side. She'd be glad when all this was over, and she could get a good night's sleep.

"Get me the money, beautiful."

Every muscle in her body tensed, and her heart leaped in her chest. She stared at the doorway but still didn't see anyone.

"I'm right here." He chuckled. "In case you're considering using that gun, just know I have a rifle aimed at that sleeping little girl. Precious, ain't she?"

His voice didn't sound like Barry Goodlow, so Kylie guessed it must be Abraham Fisher. *Come on, Luke. Where are you?* "Okay," she said, trying to keep a steady voice. "Let me get the money."

"I'd appreciate it if you'd put that gun down first."

Kylie did as he asked and laid her weapon on the other side of the barn, away from the twins. What would he do once she gave him the case? Open it or just take the container and run? She bent over and picked up the case by the handle, careful not to make a fast move.

"See there. Not only are you beautiful, but smart, too. You're a good nanny."

She listened for any sounds that would let her know Luke was nearby, but heard nothing. She stepped to the dark doorway, her palms sweaty, and held the empty case close to her leg. Should she slug him in the head?

"Hand it over real slow so I don't mistakenly think you're trying to hit me like you did Barry."

So much for that idea. She'd barely moved the case when the man snatched it from her grip.

"Thank you," he said, panting as he moved quickly. His silhouette came into view as he fumbled to unlatch the case.

Oh, no. Should she run back for her gun?

"Ky-ee."

She turned and saw Braden sitting up and rubbing his eyes. "It's okay. Go back to sleep," she said, but he didn't listen. The toddler got up, and she met him halfway across the hay-strewn floor and scooped him into her arms.

"Where's the money?" Abraham's tone had gone from playful to deadly.

She tried to swallow but the dryness in her throat made her cough. What to do now?

The man burst forward and shoved the end of the rifle into her side. "I want the money."

"Okay. It's outside," she shrieked. "I'll get it for you."

He took a step back to give her room.

Zoe still slept, so she left her there. There was no way to go for her gun with Braden in her arms and she trekked outside with the man right behind her. A trip over a rock would probably get her shot. Braden remained quiet in her grasp. She maneuvered through a clump of sunflowers to the tractor. Luke said the bills were under the lid. "The money's in—"

"Get out of my way." Abraham pushed her aside and dropped the gun to his side. "If the money's not here…"

Kylie dashed for cover. She zigzagged with Braden back to the barn, but Abraham must've been happy to see the money because he didn't shoot at them. She set Braden on the ground and grabbed her Glock.

Had Barry subdued Luke? Or maybe Abraham had taken him down before he came to the barn.

As she neared the opening, gunfire exploded in the distance. Abraham cursed from outside.

Her body shook with surprise before she darted back to the kids.

The shots had to have come from the trailer.

FOURTEEN

Sweat beaded on Luke's forehead as he stood legs apart, gun drawn. "Drop your weapon."

The lack of moonlight made the shadows even darker in the trees where he stood. His hiding place underneath the huge pecan tree couldn't be better. Someone would have to be five feet away to see him. All the lights in the trailer were off.

Barry Goodlow had stood frozen in the front yard since he'd fired his warning shot.

Over thirty minutes ago, Luke heard movement in the woods and left his hiding place to check it out. He'd followed Goodlow from the woods to the trailer.

Where was Fisher?

The van sat five yards from Goodlow, and Luke knew a mad dash for his vehicle must be tempting. "Don't think about it, Goodlow. Drop your weapon," he ordered.

Luke didn't know if Jax O'Neill was close, but earlier he'd seen movement by the front the trailer. Either another suspect had joined them, or O'Neill had arrived.

Goodlow glanced around like he was considering his options.

"Now," Luke said.

Goodlow threw his rifle to the ground and held his hands in the air. "Don't shoot."

"Walk forward and keep your hands in the air."

The man glanced around, hesitant to move.

Where was his partner? Even when they knew they couldn't get away, suspects hesitated to obey. "Walk."

The man took a few steps, but kept searching the area.

Luke didn't detect movement. He kept a lookout for a glint from a gun, a sign of motion. Anything. The trailer was in the shadows.

Suddenly, the sound of running footsteps came from somewhere behind Luke.

Goodlow dropped to his knees and gunfire lit up the night.

Luke moved behind the trunk of the tree for cover.

A man darted through the trees, gun blazing, and came to an abrupt stop beside the shed.

Pop. Pop. More shots.

And then silence.

Goodlow was still, facedown in the yard. Whether he had taken a bullet or not, Luke couldn't tell.

"Don't move." Jax O'Neill's voice carried across the yard, originating from Luke's right, near the trailer. "Throw down your weapon. You've got three armed Texas Rangers with guns pointing at you. We're short on patience and long on ammunition."

Fisher shouted, "You'll have to come and get me first."

Three Rangers?

"Drop it." Texas Ranger Randolph stepped out from behind Fisher.

The kidnapper cussed and had the sense to toss his rifle to the ground and put his hands in air. "This is all Tommy Doane's doing."

O'Neill came out from behind the house as Randolph handcuffed Goodlow. "You all right, Dryden?"

"Yeah. You could've given me warning you were here." Luke's heart was still racing. He had expected Jax to give him some sort of sign that he had arrived. It had been impossible to see with all the tree cover.

O'Neill approached the man in the yard and checked for a pulse. "This one's alive. Barely. There's also one in the trailer who's been shot."

"That'd be Tommy. Is he alive?"

"He was a while ago," Jax said.

Goodlow groaned and mumbled incoherently as sirens sounded in the distance.

As Ranger Randolph led Fisher across the yard, he said, "We'll be taking that money."

Fisher had the money. Fear choked Luke. "I need to check on Kylie and the twins."

"I'm here." Kylie's voice came from somewhere on the trail. "You could help me, though."

Luke holstered his gun and hurried to meet her. The sight of her with the twins stole his breath, a deep ache in his chest. They were all right. He strode over. Immediately he held out his hands and took Braden.

The little fellow cried. "Me wanna go home."

Luke patted his back. "It's okay. We'll take you to Grandpa and Grandma's house soon." When he tried to take Zoe, Kylie said, "I can carry one of them." Her hair hung in her face and the circles around her eyes showed her exhaustion.

He whispered in her ear, "When I heard Fisher

had the money it almost scared me half to death." His shoulders sagged as he pulled her into a hug. "Glad you and the kids are all right. Heard Goodlow tramping through the woods and I followed him back here. I never would've left if I had known Fisher was out there."

"When you didn't come out, I knew something had happened."

He pulled away from the embrace as the ambulance pulled into the drive, bright lights swirling. At least they had cut the sirens.

Kylie looked at him, her eyes full of questions. "Tommy?"

"I don't know. I haven't gone in yet." He squeezed her hand reassuringly. "Let me go check. Keep them out here. Okay?"

"Okay." She gave his shoulder one last touch before he turned around.

Luke hurried into the trailer. Tommy was sprawled out on the floor, his breathing labored. "Are you hit?"

Tommy moaned. "I am." He gasped in another breath. "Sorry...'bout this. Megan deserved better."

"Save your energy." Luke kneeled beside his brother-in-law—the pain was evident as Tommy clenched his teeth.

"Braden... Zoe." Tommy's hand grasped Luke's and squeezed, a desperate act of helplessness.

"The kids are safe. An ambulance is here to take you to the hospital. Hang in there, Tommy." Luke waited until two paramedics came through the back door carrying a stretcher.

"Over here." Luke motioned to where Tommy was lying on the floor. He stepped out of the way so the man and woman could do their jobs.

"Get Hal. Make him pay…for Megan. Video on my phone. Couch." Tommy's voice trailed behind him as Luke went to retrieve Tommy's cell phone. A quick scroll through the videos and he found the one he was looking for. Nausea swirled in his gut as Megan's image appeared. The terror in her eyes. His hands shook as he heard Alcott's voice demand the return of the money in three hours. Luke stalked down the back steps. He intended to get Alcott. The man responsible for Megan's death would not get away with it.

"How's your brother-in-law?" Jax asked.

"Doesn't look good. He took a bullet to the shoulder earlier today and now this one in his gut. He's lost a lot of blood."

Jax shook his head. "That's never good."

"We have the evidence we need to bring Alcott down." He held up Tommy's phone.

"You okay?" Jax's gaze narrowed. "What did you find?"

"I will be as soon as this man's behind bars." He handed Jax the cell phone and opened it to the video.

His buddy's eyes turned cold as he stared at the image. "I'm sorry, Dryden. We'll get him."

To process the scene would take a while. Luke scanned the yard looking for Kylie.

"Over here." Kylie's voice carried above the hum of the chaos in the yard. She had moved off to the side, out of the way of first responders.

Luke strode over.

She whispered, "How's Tommy?"

"The paramedics are with him right now." Luke took Braden from her and moved closer, even though he knew the kids wouldn't understand. "Doesn't look good."

"Is Fisher or Goodlow talking?"

"Goodlow's hurt, but he was able to mumble he didn't know what was going on. Innocent bystander."

"Innocent bystander carrying an assault rifle. Of course," she replied sarcastically.

"Fisher is throwing all the blame on Tommy. And evidently I grazed his left hand with a bullet while at the quarry."

Jax joined them. "This may take a while and the mosquitoes are awful. You want me to help the kids in the truck?"

"I got this," Luke answered. With the ambulance's light flashing across the yard and people hurrying to do their jobs, the kids were wide-awake.

"Fine," Jax said. "But I have some fruit snacks in my truck if the kids are hungry."

"Thanks." Luke nodded for Kylie to follow and they put the kids in their car seats.

Randolph walked up to the truck. "Can they have a sticker?"

At the sight of the stickers in the shape of an old Western lawman's badge, Braden and Zoe held out their hands.

Braden yelled, "I want one."

"Me, too," Zoe chimed in.

The Ranger smiled and stuck one on each of their shirts. He looked at Kylie. "I have kids of my own."

After Randolph walked away, Luke stuck his head in the door. "I'll be back shortly."

It took over an hour for information to be exchanged. When Tommy and Goodlow had left by ambulance and they were through giving their statements, Luke and Kylie drove the kids back to his parents' house.

Sam and Dottie were pacing the kitchen floor when Luke walked through the front door at four-thirty in the morning with Kylie and the twins.

"My babies." Tears ran down his mother's face as soon as her gaze landed on the kids. Even though the twins were sound asleep, he allowed his mom to take Zoe from his arms.

"I was so scared." His mom squeezed Zoe until she began to stir awake. "Grandma loves you so much." She looked up at Luke. "Thank you. Thank you so much, son."

"Uh, I'll help you, Dot." Sam didn't say a word to Luke but took Braden from Kylie. His dad's hands shook as he held his grandson. With circles under his eyes, the man seemed to have aged ten years in the last few months.

"They're awfully tired, Mom and Dad."

A slow smile came to his mom's lips, her face glowing. "We'll put the kids to bed. I'm just so happy to have them safe."

"What did the doctor say?"

His dad waved his hand through the air. "I'm fine."

"They didn't think there was a concussion, but your dad has a pretty big goose egg," his mom added. "They gave me a list of things to watch for like confusion or problems with coordination."

Dad's eyes cut toward her. "Let's get the twins to bed."

"You want something to eat?" Luke asked Kylie after his parents left the room.

"I'm starved." She held her stomach.

"Late supper or early breakfast?" He opened the refrigerator door to see what was available.

"Doesn't matter. Anything simple. There's no need to go to any trouble."

"There's chicken-fried steak and mashed potatoes in the microwave," his mom called from the bedroom.

Kylie's face grew a large smile. "She reminds me of my mom."

Luke returned the gesture. "Mom is great."

His mom shouted again, "Gravy's in the fridge."

"Thanks." Luke chuckled. "That's one thing. I've never gone hungry."

Kylie helped fill two plates and put them in the microwave. She also found sliced cantaloupe. "This looks so good."

Luke found some biscuits in the bread cupboard, while she poured a couple of glasses of sweet iced tea and set them on the table.

They were about to sit down when his folks came into the room, their eyes shining. Before Luke took a seat at the table, a hand clamped down on his shoulder. He turned around to his dad standing there.

"Thanks, son." The words were barely more than a whisper but the emotion behind them spoke volumes.

His dad wasn't a sensitive mushy type of man, and Luke knew it took a lot for his dad to make the gesture. There was something else in those dark eyes. Guilt? An apology? Luke didn't know, but his dad was trying to make amends and he wasn't about to let that slide. "You're welcome, *Dad*."

If Luke didn't know better, he'd think the moisture in those eyes were tears. He took the chair next to Kylie feeling somewhat sentimental by his dad's reaction. It was more than worry over the twins' safety, although that was certainly part of it. Regret had shown in his dad's expression. Now in the light of things, his parents withholding the fact that Sam wasn't his biological father didn't feel like such a big deal as it did a few weeks before.

He and Kylie sat at the table. She bowed her head.

Luke said grace before the meal for the first time in months.

Things seemed to be headed in the right direction. Only one thing could destroy his future plans. He shoved up his sleeves as he picked up his fork.

It was time for Hal's reckoning.

FIFTEEN

The early morning sun peeked through the blinds as Kylie and Dottie watched the kids in the living room. Braden and Zoe hadn't gotten much sleep, but you'd never know it by watching them play in the small frog-shaped tent filled with plastic balls. They were overflowing with energy. No doubt, they'd need a good nap later, but it did Kylie's heart good to see them just be kids again.

Even Zoe's quiet shell seemed to crack as she squealed and threw a ball at Braden.

Luke strode into the room. "Jax called." He leaned forward and whispered, "Tommy didn't make it."

"Oh, I'm sorry." She knew the chances had been slim, but the news still saddened her.

He straightened. "Alcott has a property on the southwest side of town in his wife's name. We're on our way with an arrest warrant for Megan's murder."

"You have enough evidence?" She didn't want to throw doubt on the good news, but she understood how easy it was for criminals to get off if the proof wasn't solid.

"Tommy gave us what we needed."

Luke's tight smile told her he'd found something he hadn't shared with her. "I want to go with you." Even as the words came out of her mouth, she knew the kids would need more protection. Look what had happened yesterday. Her heart ripped into two different directions.

He glanced at his folks and then nodded his head toward the door. Kylie followed him out to his truck. He placed his hands on her biceps and rubbed gently up and down. "I want you to stay here. Please. You know better than anyone that Hal is a dangerous man. I don't want you anywhere near him. I believe the twins are safe, but I'd feel much better if you and my family were all here together. We don't need a repeat of yesterday."

She stared into his dark eyes, emotions dancing. "I've waited for this moment for over three years, Luke. I need to see him brought down. The kidnappers are no longer a threat."

Disappointment, and maybe something else, crossed his face. Fear? "I won't stop you. You're good at your job. You've proven that over and over. I worry about you and my family's safety."

He'd lost so much already. Kylie could practically read his thoughts. He didn't want to lose her. "I—"

He leaned in and brushed his lips against hers. "Stay." She started to pull away, but his arms encircled her, pulling her against him. His lips pressed against her mouth, sweet yet urgent. Every bit of emotion was thrown in that one kiss. "Stay, Kylie."

Every nerve in her body tingled uncontrollably. Her breath was taken away. Against her will, her voice shook, and she whispered, "Luke, I'll stay with the twins. Promise me you'll be careful."

A slow smile enveloped his face. "I promise." He

opened his truck door and started to get in, but then he
stopped, turned and yanked her against him. His voice
hoarse, he said, "I want more of that."

He planted another kiss on her lips, and Kylie melted
into his arms. When he pulled away once more, he
stared deeply into her eyes. "We need to talk when I
get back."

A smile spread across her moist lips. She still felt
his touch burning as she watched him leave down the
driveway. She waited until the gate closed before going
back into the house.

Zoe was playing on the floor with a rag doll and
Braden stood on the couch. He jumped up and down
and then leaped onto the leather chair.

"Braden Michael, don't jump on the furniture." Dottie quickly crossed the room to his side.

Kylie breathed a sigh of relief. It was almost over.
There'd be a trial and all, but today was the day. Would
she really be able to see her family in the next twenty-
four hours? Surreal. She had the itch to call her sister
right now and tell them the good news. Get them prepared. Her mom, sisters and brothers. Kylie had a niece
she'd never met before—little Gracie they called her.

She plopped down on the couch happy to have a
break from it all. *Lord, please put Your protective hand
over Luke and Jax as they go to arrest Hal Alcott. I'm
ready to see my family.*

With the prayer said, a big weight lifted from her
shoulders. Never again would she take family for
granted. A vision of Luke came to her mind. The longing in his eyes. The kiss.

An image of Hal Alcott flashed. The rising smoke

from the explosion. The satisfied smirk on his face. Chills formed on her arms. *Yes, God, please be with him.*

Luke eased off the accelerator again. Known for being the patient Texas Ranger, he struggled to keep his speed down. Adrenaline wouldn't let him alone this time—too much was at stake. He was ready for this case to be closed. To get back to his family, the twins. And yes, to Kylie.

The kiss kept replaying through his mind. He didn't know what her plans were when Alcott was safely behind bars, but he hoped to be a part of her life.

He called Jax again. His partner was waiting at the gas station on the corner, a couple of miles from Alcott's country home. A few minutes later, he pulled into the lot. Sergeant Jamison and three of his officers were also waiting. They all got out of the vehicles and went over the plan one more time. The arrest needed to go off without a hitch.

Plan in place, they all pulled out in a line. Jax and Luke led, the others hung back. The name of the farm was in big metal letters—Peaceful Valley. As he came up to the tree-lined gate, colorful flowers and shrubbery dotted the drive. A large lake stood to the right in the valley and a smattering of large pecan trees completed the scene. A couple of horses and a small herd of longhorns lazily grazed on the lush grass.

For a second, doubt crept in. Hal Alcott appeared to be a successful Texas landowner. Living the American dream. But it was all a ruse, Luke knew. Success on the back of crime. Prosperous because of the mistreatment and intimidation of others.

As he pulled up to the stone home trimmed in cedar,

he spotted a Lexus parked in front of the garage, the trunk open. He and Jax got out at the same time and exchanged glances.

Luke nodded at the garage. They hoped to apprehend Hal with no injuries or trouble, but prepared for the worst. Rocky Creek police officers stopped a little farther back. Officer White had been instructed to take a back entrance to the property, and Luke detected the glint of his bumper as he drove through the pasture behind the home.

As Luke approached with his gun on his belt but the safety strap off, Hal came out of the garage, a suitcase in his hand. The man did a double take and his eyes widened. "Luke?" His voice was high-pitched. "What are you doing here?"

Luke kept his expression passive. "Hal, I need to talk with you."

His gaze went to Jax and the badge on his chest. "You're that other Texas Ranger. We met the other day. What is this?"

"I have an arrest warrant for the murder of Megan Doane." Luke held the paper out to him, but Alcott didn't take it.

Shock registered as Luke read him his Miranda rights. He glanced over Luke's shoulder, apparently seeing the police cruisers. "I'll need to speak with my lawyer."

"You have that right."

Alcott started to put the suitcase in the trunk.

"You need to put that down. We also have a search warrant."

"Now see here. Let me see that warrant."

Luke handed it to him. Jax silently stood a couple

of feet behind him, off to his left. The search warrant covered the house, barn and vehicles.

Alcott's face burned red. "I demand you explain this."

"The murder of Megan Doane and, possibly, Lori Coffey and her two children."

"Hold on. You're making a big mistake." With a trembling hand, he quickly put in a call to his lawyer while the officers fanned out and started going through his things.

After Alcott hung up, he said, "You know I wouldn't hurt your sister. I didn't even know her."

Luke remained neutral, trying not to show emotion to the man's words. Hal had always been fit and well-dressed. He could imagine most women found the businessman attractive. But today, Alcott aged ten years, the white in his hair prominent and disheveled, his shirt wrinkled and untucked. "I appreciate that."

"I have never killed anyone in my life. That's ridiculous. Not Megan, or Lori and her kids. This is a far stretch from money laundering, which I was exonerated of, by the way. You're wasting my time."

"Tommy Doane worked for you. We believe he embezzled more than a million dollars from you. You killed Megan to try to persuade Tommy to hand over the money. When that didn't work, you tried to kidnap Tommy's twin kids."

"That's ridiculous. No jury will ever believe that contrived story. Do you really think the town of Rocky Creek will convict their favorite Sunday-school teacher? The man who has provided beautiful homes to middle-class families at fair prices. I've donated to more charity events than any other citizen in the town's history." The man gained confidence the longer he talked. "I'm sorry about your sister, Dryden, but you won't find one shred of evidence to back up your accusations."

"We have a video of you with Megan tied up. We also have a witness that places you at the scene of the Coffey murders."

He sighed like that was a silly claim, but there was a slight change in his eyes. "What witness?"

Luke didn't have to explain the evidence they had against Alcott, but it was clear the man had been caught off guard and was willing to talk. Sometimes the most dangerous criminals sang like canaries when they were cornered. "Deputy United States Marshal Melody Garner places you at the scene."

"Impossible." Hal's face drained of color. "She's dead."

Luke shook his head and kept his tone light. "Oh, no, Hal. She's given her statement to the police."

Luke noted Jax had his gun in his hand and ready.

"Melody Garner's dead," Alcott repeated.

"Not hardly. She's alive and well and naming you as the killer."

Confusion etched Alcott's expression, his confidence all but gone. Then, as if something crossed his mind, he smiled. "I didn't kill the Coffey family, and I don't care what the marshal, *if* she's alive, claims she saw."

An officer came from around the back of the house. "He's been burning papers in his barbecue pit."

Luke looked back at him. "You can't get rid of the evidence."

Hal's normal suave appearance vanished. An old man stood in his place. "I didn't kill anyone. I've never personally killed anyone in my life and that's a promise.

You know me better than that, Dryden. I know your folks. Remember when they had me and Sylvia over for that cancer fund-raiser? Wasn't that your cousin's benefit?"

"It was, but that doesn't make any difference now. You can't do enough good to make up for the crimes you've committed. It doesn't work that way." Luke's impatience grew. Alcott couldn't shake his confidence that he had the right man. They needed to bring the man in and finish questioning him.

"I didn't kill the Coffey family." A sneer crossed his lips. "I'm afraid it was someone a little closer to home on this one, Ranger."

"I don't believe that, Hal. The witness places you—"

"I admit it—I was there at the scene *after* the explosion. But I didn't blow up the safe house. I came there to stop the killings because children shouldn't be murdered because of their parents. It was one of the marshals."

Luke stared at the man, afraid to speak for his own doubt might be detected.

"Assistant director of United States Marshals to be exact." Alcott smirked. "Seth Wheeler is your killer."

SIXTEEN

Kylie chewed on her lip as she waited to hear back from Luke. Several scenarios ran through her mind at a hundred miles per hour. Imagining Hal having a supply of guns and a hitman going ballistic and blowing Luke and his team away, to Hal using his charisma to convince law enforcement she had concocted the story so she wouldn't be blamed for the Coffey family's demise. She'd also pictured him peacefully being arrested and admitting to the killings.

Patience was not her strong point.

Dottie sat on the couch with the twins while they watched a popular old children's movie that Kylie had grown up watching. Sam Dryden stood in the kitchen staring out the window. A .357 Magnum sat on top of the refrigerator, out of the kids' reach. Kylie had seen Sam check the chamber right after Luke left. No doubt he was determined that no one was going to kidnap these kids ever again.

Her own Glock was secured in her ankle holster under her pant leg.

She got up from the recliner for the fifth time and went into the kitchen, adrenaline running rampant. A bowl of M&Ms sat on the counter, and she grabbed a handful. She ate them without even tasting them. A two- to three-mile run would do her good right about now. But since that was out of the question, she continued to pace through the house.

Her iPad sat on her bed and she wanted to look at the pictures of her family on Facebook again. Her mom's surgery was scheduled in two weeks. Would Kylie's sudden reappearance from the dead be too much for her mom's health? Would the surprise actually add to her issues?

As soon as Kylie got the okay from Luke, she'd call her oldest sister. Tina would let her know whether to let them know she had been rogue undercover for the last three years or wait until Mom was out of the woods.

Searching the internet could wait for another thirty minutes. Or an hour. Or three or four hours, whatever it took to arrest Hal. Luke had gone out early this morning and purchased her another phone. She checked the volume to make certain it was turned up so she wouldn't miss his call.

As she roamed back to the kitchen, a light flashed across the window. She leaned over the sink to see around Sam. A white Buick pulled to the gate.

"I don't recognize that vehicle." Sam narrowed his gaze.

Kylie watched and remained quiet, momentarily noticing there was something familiar about the driver. As the vehicle pulled to a stop, she saw the US Marshal emblem on the door. Why would one of the marshals be here?

"What is it?" Dottie stood up, leaving the twins on the couch. Kylie stepped back and gave the woman room.

"A car."

Dottie shook her head. "Do you think they could mean trouble?"

"Don't know," Sam mumbled. "And I only see one person. Looks like the US Marshals." He glanced at Kylie.

A man got out and stood at the gate, his stance familiar. He wore a pair of tan pants and a light jacket over a navy pullover shirt, almost like…

"Hold on." Kylie's stomach fluttered as she leaned closer for a better look.

"Do you know him?" Sam asked.

"That's Seth Wheeler. The assistant director of US Marshals." What was he doing here? Kylie hadn't called him. Maybe one of the Texas Rangers had. But why?

"A US Marshal?"

Kylie nodded. "Did Luke tell you I used to work for the Marshals?"

"I surmised something was going on, but Luke didn't say." Sam looked at her. "That's quite an accomplishment to put on your résumé for a nanny."

Kylie caught the subtle sarcasm.

Dottie asked, "Are you going to let him in, Sam? He's an officer."

Sam looked at Kylie, his eyebrows raised in question.

She and Luke had discussed the probability of a mole being in the US Marshals, and Wheeler may've learned something about the Coffey murders. She carefully weighed her options. Wheeler was alone and she was armed. Her boss had been an honest lawman for over twenty years and had been like a dad after she had lost her own father. "Let him in."

Sam released the automatic gate, and she watched the government-issued car pull down the drive and stop in front of the house. Kylie went out to greet her old boss. "Marshal Wheeler, what are you doing here?"

"It's good to see you, Garner. Or should I call you Kylie Stone?"

She stared at him a moment, not certain if there was animosity in his tone or just fun. Sarcasm wasn't unknown to her old boss. "Either is fine. Actually, it's been so long since anyone called me Melody Garner. It's almost foreign."

Before they stepped in the door, he said, "Being you kept your identity a secret for over three years, I'd say we taught you well."

"You certainly did. But you didn't answer my question, sir. What are you doing here? How did you know where I was?"

A strained smile crossed his lips. The older man hadn't changed a bit, except his hair was a little more gray and she detected an extra wrinkle or two. Seeing someone from her past was surreal. She was on the verge of coming out of hiding and was more than ready to live again. Her old boss wasn't used to being questioned, and Kylie was uncomfortable being forward, but she couldn't let the issue slide.

His eyes glistened, and this time his smile looked like the old Wheeler. "Your sister Tina called me."

"My sister?"

He nodded. "She thought she saw you on the news the other night. Apparently, she called local law enforcement and when they wouldn't take her seriously, she called our department. Took a day for me to get the message." He cocked his head. "I was pretty shocked when I viewed the video of the dollar store. I had to come see for myself if it was really you. We have some things to discuss. As you can imagine, I have plenty of questions about the incident with the Coffey family."

"Come on in." She couldn't wait to tell what she had witnessed and to get to the bottom of who was the mole. If there was a mole.

Sam and Dottie both waited in the kitchen for them to enter.

Kylie introduced them, and Luke's parents seemed to relax as the Marshal shook their hands.

Dottie sent him a warm smile. "Won't you have a seat at the table? I'm afraid the twins might crawl all over you if you sit in the living room."

"Thank you, but I enjoy kids. Especially since my wife and I became grandparents. We have three little grandkids of our own. Two boys and a girl between the ages of six months and four years." The man shrugged out of his jacket and laid it under the coffee table, and then he settled on the couch. "Could I trouble you for a cup of coffee?"

Braden grinned at Kylie's old boss and marched on the cushions next to him.

"Of course." Dottie went to get Wheeler some, but added, "Braden, you need to sit down on the couch."

Zoe stared at him, and after a second, climbed down and ran to Kylie.

"It's like they say." Wheeler chuckled. "If I'd known grandkids were so much fun, I would've had them first."

Kylie allowed Zoe to climb to her on the soft chair across from Marshal Wheeler, suddenly feeling like she had been called into the principal's office. She hadn't expected to see anyone from the US Marshals until Hal Alcott was in jail and she had reconnected with her family. Only then had she planned to contact the department to see what it would take to get her old job back. She figured that would be several weeks from now, but not today. Not that she didn't appreciate Wheeler's help, but she would've thought he could've simply called.

"Care to update me on what happened? What went wrong three years ago?"

Again, Kylie stared into his shining brown eyes, feeling like she was under scrutiny. Not that she blamed him. She supposed Wheeler would've taken a lot of heat for what was believed to be the death of one of his deputies, along with a family under protection. And then to learn his deputy was alive and faked her death had to irritate beyond reason. She decided to give him the short version, starting with what happened at the safe house that morning, and later how she'd seen Hal after the explosion as he looked over the scene. Then she explained the connection between him and Luke's sister.

Wheeler nodded slowly, taking it in. Dottie set a steaming cup of coffee on the end table beside him. "Ah. Thank you, Mrs. Dryden."

She smiled and then eyed the twins. No doubt Dottie hoped the kids wouldn't spill the man's drink on the carpet.

Sam hung out in the kitchen, splitting his attention between the kitchen window and their visitor.

"How's the rest of the team?" Kylie had stayed abreast of some her ex-coworkers through social media, but many of them didn't post publicly. For those who didn't participate, sometimes Kylie still stayed informed by following their spouses.

"Good. Everyone misses you, Garner. The team hasn't been the same without you. Justin, the deputy who took your place, has done a fine job but nothing as good as you."

"Thank you." Kylie had also looked up her replacement. A funny pit in her stomach developed. She had researched enough to realize Justin Pauley was the son of an old-time friend of Seth Wheeler. But she knew her boss, and he would never hire anyone on friendship alone. He was a fair leader, and a good law-enforcement officer. She wanted to ask the assistant director about the possibility of a mole being in the department, but she'd rather have someone at her side when that conversation took place. Someone like Luke.

Wheeler looked up and called out, "That was some good coffee, Mrs. Dryden. I didn't mean to interrupt your day."

"That's quite all right." Dottie came in and sat on the fire hearth. Sam stepped into the room and leaned against the wall. It didn't escape Kylie's attention he could still view the kitchen window from his vantage point.

Tina had seen her on television? The thought kept crossing her mind. Did her sister tell the rest of the family? Being that Tina put out the effort to get in contact with the US Marshals meant she probably tried to find Kylie herself. If her family thought she was alive, there was nothing holding Kylie back from calling them. As soon as Wheeler left, she'd contact them even if Luke hadn't returned by then.

"What are the kids' names?"

Dottie said, "Zoe and Braden."

Wheeler called the twins. "If it's all right with your grandmother, I have some candy." He held out two suckers.

Zoe and Braden's eyes lit up.

"I want one." Braden leaped to the floor in front of Wheeler.

Her old boss ruffled the top of Braden's head. "I always carry treats for kids now that I'm getting older."

Dottie's hesitant smile told Kylie the woman would rather the twins not have the sweets, but she gave in, anyway. "That'll be fine."

Braden snatched the blue one out of the man's hand, ripped off the paper and threw it to the floor.

Zoe watched, but stayed where she was.

Wheeler held out the candy. "You want it? Come get it."

The little girl looked to Dottie for reassurance. After her grandmother nodded, Zoe eased away from Kylie. She held out her hand for the sucker while still standing a couple of feet away.

Wheeler laughed. "Here you go."

When Zoe stepped closer, Wheeler reached out and pulled the toddler to him and then grabbed Braden.

US Marshal Wheeler pointed to Sam and said in a deadly serious tone, "Now you can sit next to your wife. Melody, don't make a move for your weapon or... else." He tilted his head toward the twins. "And come sit by me."

Kylie froze, trying to process what she was seeing. Slowly her heart seized, as realization slammed into her. She opened her mouth to speak, but nothing came out. Never in her nightmares had she suspected her boss of betrayal.

Luke stared at the man he once believed a great leader of the community and watched as a sly smile crept up Alcott's lips. Luke drew a deep breath. "You're saying Melody Garner's boss is the one who leaked the family's location?"

"No. I'm saying he's the one who planted the explosive. He takes a cut on every large crooked deal he can. Money laundering. Drug crimes. Racketeering. You name it. He only plays with big money. He wasn't about to see me go down three years ago. But when an important job needs to be done right, the man does the hit himself. Wheeler made certain Deputy US Marshal Garner was the only law enforcer on the premises."

The knot in Luke's stomach grew stone hard as he tried to digest the information. "What about Megan?"

"I don't even remember what your sister looked like, Dryden. Someone stole over a million dollars from me and someone had to die." Alcott shrugged like it was a matter of circumstance. "It's just the way the game's played. Nothing personal."

Red-hot heat rushed through Luke's body as his pulse raced. His fists clenched. It took everything in his being not to pulverize the slimeball.

Kylie. At the thought, he sucked in a sharp breath. The twins and his parents. All alone and thinking the danger was far from them.

He spun. "O'Neill. I need to go."

Sergeant Jamison said, "I've got this, Dryden."

Luke didn't hesitate and ran to his truck when O'Neill yelled, "I'm with you. Randolph can finish here."

He didn't argue but got in his truck and peeled out of the drive. He hit Kylie's number. "Please answer." Four rings and then it went to voice mail. He turned onto the highway and tried again. "Come on, Kylie. Where are you?"

When neither of his parents answered, fear really

settled in. Hopefully they were all just busy playing outside with the kids or something and didn't hear their phones, but he didn't think so. A hard pit formed in his stomach the size of Texas as he broke every speed limit on the road.

A glance to his rearview mirror showed Jax not far behind him.

Doom settled on his shoulders as he realized he was still thirteen miles away.

Please, God, keep my family and Kylie safe. I should've never left them alone. I messed up. I'll never doubt You again if You'll just get me through this.

Let me get there in time.

SEVENTEEN

With the barrel of Wheeler's .357 Magnum jabbed into her temple, Kylie forced herself to remain calm. She sat next to Wheeler, the twins in his lap. There had to be a way out of this. Sam's gun sat on the top of the refrigerator. Hers was still in her holster. Wheeler kept a firm grip on Zoe and Braden, and she needed to get them away from him.

With his left hand, the marshal retrieved zip ties from his back pocket and tossed them at Luke's mom. "Secure your husband to the chair."

Dottie sent him a glare that would frighten most seasoned warriors and moved to do his bidding without a word.

"Oh, wait. What was I thinking?" Wheeler talked politely almost to the point of sounding silly. "Mr. Dryden raise your shirttail and your pants leg. I hope you don't have any weapons on you. Might be harmful to the little ones."

Sam never said a word as he lifted his shirt to show he had no guns there and then removed a pistol from an ankle holster.

"Put it on the kitchen table and then move that dining chair over there and sit." He indicated the other side of the room, across from the couch.

Kylie had thought his only weapon was in the kitchen. Smart man. Too bad he hadn't been able to use it to subdue her old boss.

Kylie's cell phone vibrated in her back pocket. Luke was the only one with her number.

Wheeler shook his head. "Don't even think about answering that."

"Let me down." Braden held an empty sucker stick in his hand and squirmed against Wheeler's hold.

"Easy, little fella." Wheeler adjusted his grip.

"No!" Braden struggled against being held. "I want down."

Zoe watched her brother and evidently didn't like seeing him upset. She burst into tears.

Fearing Wheeler might hurt the toddlers, Kylie asked, "Do you have any more candy?"

"No." The man looked back at Luke's parents. "You may secure him to the chair now."

Kylie believed Sam would kill Wheeler if given the chance. The sharp look, the working of his jaw. Veins bulging in his neck, Sam fumed as his wife tightened the thick plastic to his wrists.

And just like Kylie, Sam was helpless as long as Wheeler used the kids as his armor.

Zoe's lip puckered as she tried to get away and run to Kylie, but Wheeler held her back. "Nuh-uh. Stay with me, little one."

Braden frowned and shook his fists. "Let me go."

The marshal laughed. "You're a feisty one, aren't you?"

"Don't hurt him, Marshal Wheeler." Kylie purposely

called him "Marshal," hoping it would sink in what he was doing. She'd worked with this man for six years. Surely there was good down deep inside of the veteran lawman.

He smiled. "I'll make sure the kids are safe as long as you three do as you're asked."

After Sam's wrists were tied behind his back and secured to the chair, Wheeler used the gun to point at Dottie. "Melody, your turn. Tie her up."

"Ky-ee," Braden yelled.

"Oh, wait. Wait. Wait." The marshal chuckled. "Your gun." He indicated her ankle. "Remove it real slow and toss it into the fireplace."

Her heart seized as she looked at the twins, fear and confusion etched across their little faces. She had to save them. She did as Wheeler asked and threw her Glock over the back of the couch into the hearth.

"Your cell, too."

She did as she was told.

A satisfied smile crossed his dry lips. "I knew you'd be carrying. I taught you well, young lady. I'm sorry it had to come to this. You made a feisty deputy."

She ignored the man and turned to the kids. "It's okay, Braden. Kylie's right here. Uncle Luke will be here in a minute."

"Don't count on it. He's busy arresting Hal Alcott. The businessman won't go quietly, and he has an awesome lawyer. Will be some time before the Texas Ranger is back." The marshal shook his head. "I don't like this, Garner. You know that. You've left me with no choice. You would've been better off to die in that explosion."

"I tried to protect innocent people so they could

testify. Sorry that inconvenienced you." Keep him talking. Luke could be here anytime, no matter what Wheeler claimed. With all the weapons out of reach, Kylie couldn't think of a way to overtake the marshal without risking the twins' safety. And as laid-back as the man appeared, he was no rookie and she couldn't count on him making a mistake.

Were Luke and Jax on their way? *Please, Lord, let help arrive soon.*

"Her chair goes there, at least three feet from Mr. Dryden's."

Kylie grabbed the zip ties and dragged a chair across the room. After Dottie took the seat, Kylie gently pulled her arms behind her back. The older woman furrowed her brow and her eyes grew large.

What? Kylie did a double take. Again, Dottie looked at her and quickly glanced at the ground. Then she repeated the sequence. She was trying to tell her something.

As she secured the woman to the back of the ladder-back chair, Kylie noticed something protruding under Dottie's khaki pants. A gun?

Kylie didn't pull the ties too tight, hoping Dottie might wriggle free, yet tight enough that Wheeler didn't notice. "I see it," she whispered close to her ear.

"Grandma," Zoe cried and held out her arms. The precious thing rarely talked, and Kylie felt sick. The kids needed to get away from Wheeler so she could use the gun. Since he wouldn't let them go, Kylie decided to use them as a distraction instead. She held out her hands. "Come here, Zoe."

Wheeler shook his head. "No way. You know better, Melody."

Zoe and Braden both screamed.

With Wheeler's eyes on them, Kylie bent over and retrieved a Sig P232 out of Dottie's holster and slid it in the back of her waistband. She wanted to use it against the marshal, but with the twins in his clutches, the danger was too great.

"Get yourself a chair and put it over there." He pointed between Sam and Dottie.

She did as he asked, making sure her shirt covered the weapon.

Wheeler removed two more zip ties from his pocket.

"Bad man," Braden yelled and wrestled out of Wheeler's grip. Zoe watched her brother and joined in the chorus of screams.

Braden ran to Kylie, panicked and furious. "Hold me. Hold me."

She wrapped her arms around the little guy. "It's all right, Braden."

Wheeler kept Zoe in his grasp. "A good deputy never puts a civilian at risk."

Sam said, "You won't get away with this. Our son will catch you."

"I don't have time to sit around and chat." He shook Zoe, knocking her head back. "Hold still."

Kylie's fists clenched. "Stop!"

"Leave her alone," Sam roared. He yanked on the ties that bound his hands.

Dottie pleaded. "Don't hurt my baby."

"Tell 'em to be quiet then."

With a trembling voice, Luke's mom said, "Children, use your inside voices."

The marshal strode over to Kylie and kneeled behind her, setting Zoe between his legs. He yanked her arms behind her, causing pain to shoot up her shoulder, and secured her wrists with a zip tie. She had tried to keep her hands apart to create slack but didn't know if it would be enough. Immediately after Wheeler stepped away, she went to work trying to get the gun out.

Her boss finally let Zoe go, then retrieved his jacket from under the coffee table and placed it on the dining table. After gathering Kylie's gun from the fireplace and Sam's from the table, he slid them into a pocket of the jacket. "Wouldn't want the children to get hurt."

The Sig slid into her hand, and then it slipped. She caught the pistol before it fell. Hard plastic cut into her skin, but she wrangled the gun until she gripped the handle in her palm. With her hands behind her, she'd have to aim high or the bullet would hit the floor.

"Might want to say your goodbyes." Wheeler set an explosive in the center of the kitchen table, out of reach of the kids. Set a timer.

The numbers *2:00* glowed in red indicating they only had two minutes.

"Adios." Wheeler waved. "Sorry, guys."

"Take the kids," Dottie yelled. "Get them out of the house."

Still attached to the chair, Sam lunged to his feet and flew across the room. He crashed into Wheeler's legs, sending the man sprawling into the kitchen counter, and the chair broke into pieces.

The twins screamed and clung to Dottie.

Kylie twisted around as Wheeler came to his feet and made for the door. She had a clear line of fire. Bending over as far as she could, she aimed high and pulled the trigger. Being in an awkward position, the recoil knocked her to the floor.

Pop. The shot echoed through the house.

The assistant director of the US Marshals crumpled to the floor clutching his hip. "You shot me!"

"Let's get out of here." Sam struggled to his feet, the zip tie dangling from his arm. He removed a knife from his pocket and ran to his wife.

The bomb now read *1:05.*

Zoe and Braden. She had to save the kids. Kicking and jerking, she tried to free herself of the chair, but she couldn't get loose.

"Kylie." Luke filled the doorway. When his gaze lit on her, his face paled as he ran to her side. He slid a knife from his pocket.

"Get the kids out," Kylie pleaded. "There's a bomb!"

"Jax will get them." He cut her ties and her arms fell free.

She looked up just as Jax got the kids and Luke's parents out the front door. Luke pulled her to her feet. "Come on."

The red numbers read *0:14.*

She glimpsed Seth Wheeler propped against the sink, a gun in his hand. "Back door," she shrieked and dashed for the exit.

Gunfire exploded.

She fell to the ground and crawled as her gaze sought out Luke. He was right behind her.

Boom! An explosion slammed her face into the ground. Burning heat encompassed her. And an eerie silence.

Debris fell around her.

No. Not again. This couldn't be happening. Had the children gotten far enough away?

* * *

Black smoke billowed around him. Luke was lying in the back door. A loud ringing reverberated through his ears. Despite the excruciating pain, he forced himself to his feet. Kylie. Stumbling, he ran, trying to get his bearings. Amidst the smoke, he could see his parents' house still standing. "Kylie?"

Staggering across the yard, he saw her, and his heart constricted. She was lying in the grass, gagging and choking. And she was alive. "Are you okay?"

She coughed once more before she nodded. "My ears are ringing, but other than that, I think I'm fine." She swiped at her eyes and blinked. "Is it you?"

He smiled. "Of course, it's me. Let's get you out of here."

"Luke. Kylie." His dad's voice boomed across the yard. "Are you all right?"

She struggled to sit. "I think so."

Luke looked up as his dad rushed to their sides.

The older man's gaze took them both in, relief in his eyes. "Son, you're all right, too?"

"Banged up a little." And he realized in that moment, Sam Dryden would be the only dad he ever needed. As much as it hurt to be deceived, his parents had always loved him. They'd made mistakes, but being a father to Luke wasn't one of them. "Mom and the twins make it out safely?"

He nodded. "Everyone is safe except for the marshal. Wheeler didn't make it."

Luke bent down and helped Kylie to her feet.

She buried her face into his chest, and he breathed in the feel of her. Never had anyone felt so right in his life. He could cradle her in his arms like this forever.

Luke felt more than saw his dad walk away. For a few moments he simply held Kylie, neither saying a word, only the sound of their breathing.

Sirens wailed in the distance.

She looked up into his eyes, and softly said, "Thank you."

The words were simple, but her expression told him much more. "No. Sweetheart, you're the one who helped me through this. Not just saving the twins, but helping me see my dad for what he is. I'd been fighting everyone."

"And am I finally free?" she whispered. Fatigue was clear in her face. "What happened to Hal?"

"He's been arrested for Megan's murder. He claims Wheeler committed the killings of Lori Coffey and her two kids, but it will take some digging to find out the truth and all the players. With Wheeler dead and Alcott in jail, you're free."

Kylie released a sigh and looked away. "I can go back to my family and to being Melody Garner. Who is that person?"

His hand lifted her chin, making those beautiful blue eyes connect with his. "I've never met Melody, but if she's anything like Kylie, I'd..." Even sprinkled with dirt, her pink lips called his name. He bent down and kissed her showing her how much she meant to him. Nothing or no one had ever felt so right. She sank into his arms, into his embrace. For a moment, they stood there, simply holding on to each other.

He didn't want this to end. "Before I chicken out, I need to tell you what you've done for me."

"Luke—"

He placed a finger against her lips. "No. Hear me

out." He removed his finger and took her hands into his. Kylie squeezed his hand in return. "I know I haven't been easy to get along with. You've helped more than anyone should have with Zoe and Braden. I want more. I realize you've got a family. I'd never ask you to give them up. Or your job. But I'd really like to get to know you better."

She smiled, and it almost undid him. "I gave you plenty of reasons not to trust me and you were grieving your sister's death. I hid the truth from you, but you stuck by my side and continued to investigate. You made me believe in my ability again, believe in myself."

His chest swelled, glad he'd been able to help her.

Jax came around the corner of the house carrying his cell phone, and interrupted them. "Dryden, Lieutenant Adcock wants to talk to you."

"Give me a sec." Nothing was going to stop him from what he had to say. Luke turned to Kylie and pulled her close. "Kylie Stone. Melody Garner. I don't care what you call yourself, I love you." He planted a firm kiss on lips, savoring the taste of her, and then broke contact.

Out of the corner of his eye, he saw Jax spin on his heel and disappear back around the house.

A smile stretched across Kylie's face and her eyes glistened. "You love me?"

He'd never been good at expressing himself and maybe he was making a fool of himself, but he needed her to understand. "I realize I haven't known you long, but I feel like I've known you forever. When I realized Wheeler was at the house, I'd never been so scared in my life. I was afraid I'd lost you. I don't want to go through that again. You'll want to see your family, but please don't let this be the end to us."

She continued to smile. "I've got another secret."

"Oh, no. What's that?"

"I'm not that easy to get rid of. I love you, too."

EPILOGUE

Five weeks later

Melody sat in her old place at the dining table, the noise from her family filling the room. Her mom ran into the room carrying a platter of ham and set it in front of her. She had aged a bit since Melody had gone undercover, but some of that was due to her health problems.

"Let me help you, Mom," she offered and stood.

"Nonsense. Sit down. This may be hard to believe, but I enjoy working." Her mom whisked back into the kitchen, grabbed a few more dishes and then took her seat at the table.

Tina clinked her fork on her glass. "Excuse me. Could I have everyone's attention? I just want to say we're so blessed to have everyone around the supper table again. First, Melody was brought back from the dead, and second, Mom's surgery was a success. Welcome home."

Her mom smiled. "Thanks, Tina. It's wonderful to be home. Doug, would you say grace?"

Everyone held hands, five siblings plus her mom, while Melody's brother blessed the food. As soon as he said "amen," her family dug into the food and the room filled with laughter and chatting.

Melody knew it didn't make sense, but loneliness continued to fill her. Things were going better than she ever hoped for. Her mom had recovered from the surgery and completed therapy. The doctors believed they'd removed all the cancer. A follow-up CAT scan had been scheduled in three months to monitor the progress. As much as she hated to admit it, her mom didn't need her help, at least not daily.

All of her family had been shocked but blissfully happy she was alive. Strange hearing so many people call her Melody. As happy as she was to be back, a sadness crept over her at the loss of Kylie. Who was she and where did she fit in?

"Mel, pass the biscuits."

"What?" She glanced up and found everyone staring at her.

Ben grinned. "The biscuits…"

"Oh." She smiled and handed her younger brother the bread.

"You're a million miles away, sis," Doug spouted. He stared at her a minute. Always her champion when she was a little kid. He taught her how to throw a football and even to shoot a gun. Now he had two daughters of his own.

"I figure her distraction has something to do with that handsome Ranger." Emma, just seventeen, giggled. "He needs to get on social media."

"He's a private type of guy." Melody passed the butter without having to be asked. The old family habits had returned to her almost immediately after moving back. "Luke's a nice guy."

Tina burst out laughing. "Seriously? 'Luke's a nice guy,'" she mimicked. "He's hot and you know it."

"Tina…" Melody shook her head.

Her mother said, "Don't be crude, young lady."

"I'm twenty-nine, Mom. Not exactly a kid anymore."

Melody appreciated her mom's interruption. Honestly, it was great to be home again. But if so, why did it feel like something was missing? Maybe she just needed a little more time. Braden and Zoe had stolen her heart more than she wanted to admit.

Emma leaned forward on her elbows. "So when are we going to meet this Texas Ranger?"

"He has work and twins to take care of." A lump formed in Melody's throat. She had her life back and was happy. This is what she'd wanted. Isn't it?

"So, big brother, what's this I hear about a job promotion?" Ben asked.

"Nothing's for certain yet." Doug launched into a conversation he'd had with his boss two days ago.

Melody wasn't really listening and was glad for the change in topic. She ate her food, but had a difficult time concentrating with wondering what Luke and the twins were up to. She stood and gave her mom a kiss on the cheek. "Lunch was great, Mom."

She wandered outside and sat on the back-porch swing. The sounds of her family inside the house drifted out to her. She couldn't do this. Couldn't just sit here. Too much energy. Where did she fit in? Several people from the US Marshals had called her to tell her how glad they were that she was back. She'd been offered her former job as Deputy US Marshal, and she had promised to give them an answer by tomorrow.

What was she waiting on? Undoubtedly, she should

go back to work. She'd be almost two hours from Rocky Creek. Of course, she could transfer districts and be a short commute from Luke's hometown. He had called daily and come to visit a couple of times and once while her mom was in the hospital, but she was still restless. She would go back to the Marshals. There was no need to wait until tomorrow. She'd call them right now. She dug in her pocket for her phone.

Her sister yelled something, but Melody was too preoccupied.

"Ky-ee. Ky-ee."

The little voices caused her to jerk around.

Luke was striding toward her in his boots and cowboy hat, along with the twins.

Her heart swelled with joy. She didn't wait for them, but ran to meet them. "Braden. Zoe. Oh, I'm so glad you came to see me." She dropped to her knees and gave them a hug. Both of them kept their hands behind their backs. "I've missed you."

"We brought you something," Braden yelled.

Zoe grinned. "Yeah."

Melody glanced up at Luke. "Oh, really. What did you bring me?"

Braden and Zoe whipped out a handful of daisies from behind their backs.

"Oh." She gathered the flowers together in her hands. "They're beautiful. I love them."

Luke stared down at her, his eyes connecting with hers. "So you got everything figured out yet?"

She came to her feet. "What do you mean?"

His lips curled upward into a grin. "Your family. Me and the twins. We've missed you, but you needed time to reconnect with your old life. When we were working the case, you had a lot on your plate, and I didn't want to pressure you. Are you ready to move forward? I need you to be certain because I want it all."

She smiled. "What does that mean?"

"First, I have something for you. Actually, I have two things, but this one first." His gaze held a mysterious gleam as he pulled an envelope from his back pocket.

Curiosity swept through her, but she remained silent waiting for him to explain.

"This one is for you and your mom."

"My mom?"

He handed her the envelope. "A vacation package for two to Niagara Falls."

Her heart melted and her hand, clutching the gift, went to her chest. "You remembered." Unbidden tears sprang to her eyes. "Oh, this is the sweetest thing anyone has ever done!"

"And this one…" He slid a small box from his shirt pocket as he went down to one knee.

Her throat went dry and her knees shook.

"I love you, Melody, and I want you to be my wife. The whole package. Be a mom to these two ornery kids and let's spend the rest of our lives getting to know each other."

"I love you, too." She looked into his hopeful expression and realized she wasn't complete without him. "Yes. I'll marry you."

Cheers sounded from the porch.

She laughed. "You sure you know what you're getting yourself into?"

He scooped the twins into his arms, along with her. "Like I said, I want it all."

* * * * *

Uncover the truth in thrilling stories of faith in the face of crime from Love Inspired Suspense.

Look for six new releases every month, available wherever Love Inspired Suspense books and ebooks are sold.
Find more great reads at www.LoveInspired.com

Dear Reader,

I'm so excited you could be part of my debut novel with Luke Dryden and Kylie Stone. Luke has been dealing with trust issues since he learned his parents kept a secret from him his entire life. Kylie is in hiding and keeps her true identity a secret. It takes protecting Luke's twins and fighting to stay alive to realize what is truly important.

Have you ever been in a situation where you built a wrongdoing into gigantic proportions and struggled to forgive? Have you ever done something you wished you could take back, but couldn't? I hope you can relate to Luke and Kylie's story and you can overcome like they do. Thank you for allowing me to share my story with you.

Connie Queen

Get 4 FREE REWARDS!

We'll send you 2 FREE Books plus 2 FREE Mystery Gifts.

Love Inspired Suspense books showcase how courage and optimism unite in stories of faith and love in the face of danger.

FREE Value Over $20

LOVE INSPIRED
INSPIRATIONAL ROMANCE

UPLIFTING STORIES OF FAITH, FORGIVENESS AND HOPE.

———————————

Join our social communities to connect
with other readers who share your love!

Sign up for the Love Inspired newsletter
at **LoveInspired.com** to be the first
to find out about upcoming titles,
special promotions and exclusive content.

———————————

CONNECT WITH US AT:

f Facebook.com/LoveInspiredBooks

𝕏 Twitter.com/LoveInspiredBks

Facebook.com/groups/HarlequinConnection